'You may be a god in India, but here you have a lot to learn about manners, Dr Riviero.'

He let go her arms, but did not move away from her, their bodies parallel. 'I do not need friends—the world is my friend. I am appalled at the complacency of people here. I still wonder at the miracle of being able to eat every day. May God keep me from ever showing greed! I do not need friends—not here.'

'Everybody needs friends. I've never before met anyone so arrogant that they thought they didn't. Are you so perfect, then, that you can stand alone?'

In the silence between them the waves slashed at the grey sand, and the bathers laughed and whooped. Hannah stood at the edge of the verandah, where the bougainvillea was trying to flourish in the dry soil. Ramón Riviero stood behind her, and the warmth of his body was almost painful as she recognised her desire to turn to him. His voice now was just a murmur in her consciousness. 'I was wrong earlier. I do not hate you, Hannah Day, only my own feebleness.'

She knew she must take charge of this situation before he did. In spite of his illness he was not a weakling. She took a deep breath, and swung round . . . only to find his arms already around her, locked as though that was the only place for them to be . . .

Lancashire born, Jenny Ashe read English at Birmingham, returning thence with a BA and RA—the latter being rheumatoid arthritis, which after barrels of various pills, and three operations, led to her becoming almost bionic, with two manmade joints. Married to a junior surgeon in Scotland, who was born in Malaysia, she returned to Liverpool with three Scottish children when her husband went into general practice in 1966. She has written non-stop after that—articles, short stories and radio talks. Her novels just had to be set in a medical environment, which she considers compassionate, fascinating and completely rewarding.

Jenny Ashe has written eight other Doctor Nurse Romances, the most recent being *The Partnership*, *Surgeon in the Clouds* and *Sister at Greyrigg*.

THE SURGEON FROM SAN AGUSTIN

BY

JENNY ASHE

MILLS & BOON LIMITED
ETON HOUSE 18–24 PARADISE ROAD
RICHMOND SURREY TW9 1SR

*First published in Great Britain 1987
by Mills & Boon Limited*

© Jenny Ashe 1987

*Australian copyright 1987
Philippine copyright 1987*

ISBN 0 263 75968 7

Set in 10 on 10 pt Linotron Times
03–0188–62,700

*Photoset by Rowland Phototypesetting Limited
Bury St Edmunds, Suffolk
Made and printed in Great Britain by
William Collins Sons & Co Limited, Glasgow*

CHAPTER ONE

THE MAN slammed the door of the Alfa-Sud, making dust fly. He flung his cotton jacket over one shoulder, tossed a lock of dark hair from his face, and turned to walk down the stony track towards the village hospital. It was a single-storey white building, set in a hollow. There was a Red Cross flag on the roof. From the back of the building was a view of the Canaria coastline—drab grey cliffs plunging into emerald sea.

The girl sat on the steps of the hospital, out of the sun, picking the stalks from a basket of strawberries. Her fingers were streaked with red juice. Her brown hair hung round her shoulders and hid part of her face as she worked, humming to herself. She wore a brown cotton dress with a full skirt, and her legs were wide apart, the basket between them on the step. Her feet were bare and covered with the grey dust that covered everything in San Agustín. The cement factory further round the coast sent up its own particular white dust too. And the endless fleet of aged lorries driving round past the hospital to the building sites of new hotels further round the coast, left the air full of choking fumes.

She heard a stone click against another in the shimmering heat of the afternoon. A small lizard flickered its tongue and scuttled away into the shade. Hannah looked up from her strawberries and put back a strand of hair so that she could see better. The stranger who approached had dark eyes, dark as the night, brooding and angry in the olive face. He was lean—almost thin, though the muscles in his shoulders and arms were strong and wiry. He walked with the sensual grace of a mountain lion.

The stony path led only to the hospital; he must be needing medical help. Hannah put the stalks back into the basket of strawberries and watched him curiously and with some admiration. Why was he coming here? This was a humble place, used by peasants and hotel

5

workers. He looked, in spite of his casual dress, a man of style. And his car, parked just off the road in a patch of scrub and cactus, was new and expensive.

The scrunch of stones grew louder. He strode down the path and stopped right in front of Hannah, his legs straddled, his gaze long and insolent. A single finch fluttered in the scrub behind him, but apart from that the afternoon was hushed, lazy, as though time were standing still. She looked up, her grey eyes as cool and insolent as his. He didn't walk as though he were ill, yet his face showed signs of being thinner than it should be, his trousers loose at the waist.

'*Buenas tardes, señorita.*' A harshness in his tone spoiled what could have been a warm attractive voice.

'*Buenas tardes.*'

'*Inglesa?*'

'*Si.*'

'You work here?'

'*Si.*'

'So you know a Dr Day?'

'I do.'

The man slung his jacket from his shoulders and leaned against the blinding white wall of the hospital. He suddenly looked tired, and Hannah half rose. He gestured her not to get up. 'Tell me about Dr Day. You like him? Is he a good doctor? Is he attractive to women, would you say?'

Hannah took a dislike to him then. Coolly she said, 'Colleagues don't have to be attractive, *señor*. Only efficient.'

The man looked more carefully into her face with half-closed eyes. 'So, *señorita*, you have spirit. Maybe you cheer up Dr Day in his spare time, huh? I think you do a good job.'

Hannah's voice was dangerously quiet. 'No one asked you to come here. If you have nothing better to say, there's a hospital in Las Palmas.'

'It is San Agustín I want.' He took a paper from his pocket, and sighed, murmuring almost to himself, '*Si, quiero San Agustín.*' Again he looked suddenly weary.

Rude though he was, she was concerned at the change

in his face. 'You'd better come in and sit down for a while. I'll get you some water.'

'*Agua?*' he spat out the word. 'This desalinated liquid you get here *no es potable*.'

'Then sit down anyway. You look ill.'

'No.' He spoke curtly. 'I am not a patient, *mujer*.' 'Woman.' Hannah's eyes were curtained now, on guard against further insults. He went on, his hand supporting him against the wall, 'Please do not patronise me. I will see your Dr Day and get my business over with. Then you will come with me and show me which of these tourists' bars has decent beer.' Hannah made no sign that she had heard his words, appalled at his abrupt and ungracious manner. He seemed to sense this, and added grudgingly, '*Por favor?*'

She said quietly, 'What is your business with Dr Day?'

'That I will tell to him,' he snapped.

Hannah turned back to her strawberries. She was naturally tolerant, but she disliked bullies, and this man's attitude brought out her keen resentment. The red juice had dried on her fingers. She stood up, the fruit in one hand, and turned to go indoors, ignoring the visitor. The man took a step towards her, stumbled and almost fell, clinging to the wall with desperate hands.

She dropped the strawberries in order to catch him. He was heavier than he looked, six foot against her five foot, but she managed to prevent him hitting his head on the steps. He shook his head like a boxer who had been hit. She put her arm round his waist, pulled his limp arm over her shoulder. His body was hard and firm, with no fat anywhere. 'You'd better come inside.' She helped him up the three steps and into the quiet cool of her consulting room. She led him gently to the couch and laid him there, where he stayed without moving. Hannah drew the blinds to keep the sun from his face, and brought some water from the jug in the fridge. Some she soaked a cloth with, to lay across his forehead; the rest she poured into a glass to put to his lips. She helped him raise his head. He drank the hated water without protest, and she found herself admiring his aristocratic profile, the finely shaped cheekbone and jaw.

To hide her embarrassment as he suddenly opened those black eyes and gazed directly at her, she put the water down and went back to the front steps to retrieve his jacket from the dust. Her strawberries were ruined, caked in dust and trampled into the hot baked path. She came back with the jacket, to find him already sitting up, his long legs dangling. 'I'm OK now.' He brushed aside her protest and flung the damp cloth from his forehead.

'I'll be the judge of that. Lie down, please.'

Hannah's tone was sharp. To her surprise, he obeyed her, lying down again as though he really were ill. She went to the washbowl and scrubbed the red fruit stains from her hands. Then she dried them thoroughly, and turned to take a white coat from behind the door. She put it on over the brown peasant dress and took a stethoscope from one pocket. 'Unbutton your shirt.' She took hold of the wrist that was nearest to her, slim, brown and elegant, and felt for the pulse. 'Tachycardia. Please keep very still. I'd better make a note of this. What's your name?' She reached for a patient card.

'I am Ramón Riviero. What is yours?'

'I'm Dr Day—Hannah Day.'

There was a snort of resentment from the couch. 'You? They did not tell me . . .' He took a deep breath and sat up against the pillow, shaking his head in disbelief. 'They send me to a woman!'

'Well, I'm not a gorilla, Señor Riviero. Who sent you anyway?'

He lay back as though giving in. His black eyes were intense with either anger or passion—or both. 'Pablo Rodriguez, the chief consultant at Las Palmas Hospital. You know him?'

'Very well. I play tennis with his wife Dolores. She's a Sister at the hospital.' Hannah took his wrist again, checked the pulse with her watch, then filled in the heart rate on the card. 'I need your address.'

Ramón Riviero snatched the card with a single strong movement of the wrist she had just been holding. He tore it into two, and flung both pieces on the floor. 'I am not a patient, I told you. I am fully aware of my heart rate, blood pressure and the state of my lungs. I also know exactly why I tend to feel lightheaded at times. There is a biochemical problem with my blood, and there is nothing you can do to alter that.'

'What problem?' asked Hannah.

'Never mind, it is no matter. I came to see you about something else. Pablo Rodriguez studied with me at Madrid Medical School.'

'You're a doctor?'

'I am a sugeon—was.' His handsome face clouded. 'My illness—it has been very weakening, and I am not yet back to normal life. Pablo told me you needed a second *medico* here—he told me to drive out and ask Dr Day for the job. To ask—you—for work.' The expression on his face showed how appalled he was to have to ask someone he presumed to be a peasant girl for work.

Hannah tried to remain logical. 'I do need someone here. It's hard work in mid-season. But I can't think why on earth Pablo thought you would be suitable. You hate the place, you hate the water, and you presumably hate me—at least as a colleague.'

'Right on all counts.'

'Then please tell me what you're doing here, Dr Riviero?'

'I'll try.'

There was a world of experience in his face at that moment, and in spite of his attitude towards her, Hannah couldn't help being curious. She said, 'Come through to the verandah—it's more comfortable. You'd better have a cup of tea before you go.' There was no need to part as enemies. She took off her white coat and hung it on the peg behind the door. 'You really don't want the job, do you? You would have controlled your bad temper if you did.'

He swung himself from the couch and followed her to the verandah at the back of the building. Hannah liked it, because there was a view of the beach, and it was nice to hear the thunder of the breakers, smell the freshness of the ocean rather than inhale the dust from the cement factory. He said as they walked out into the sun, and took chairs overlooking the beach, 'This is very strange to me. I have spent all my life in what you call the Third World. I was first in Ethiopia, where I was injured by a mine. Then I went out to a small village in India, where I have been for ten years. I am thirty-five years old, and never intended to return to San Agustín. But a small Indian parasite has more power than I thought, and my life may be nearer its end than it appears. Eosinophilia.'

Hannah was appalled. 'Is there cardiac involvement?'

'Yes.'

She was silent for a moment. 'Recovery is possible.'

'It is possible.'

'Do you want to go back to India?'

'I am desperate to. That is where I am needed—not here, handing out belly-ache pills and hangover cures to spoiled tourists.'

'You make yourself very clear.' She went indoors to put the kettle on. She put out the best cups. In spite of his contemptuous attitude, she still wanted to impress him —and hated herself for it. He was so very masculine, aggressively assertive. Yet behind it was something which attracted her quite violently—an underlying sensuousness that made her body respond to him while her heart and mind never could.

She carried the tray out, trying not to look at his lean long form stretched out on the chair, legs straddled in front of him. When she turned after pouring the tea she saw that his eyes had been following the line of her body in the brown dress. He didn't look away when she caught his eye, merely said, 'Why do you dress like a peasant?'

'That's what I am. My grandmother was a mill girl in the cotton mill. My father did better for himself. He started by growing vegetables on his allotment, then he managed to buy his own greengrocer's business. And I was able to go to university.' Hannah waited until he indicated milk rather than lemon, and passed him the cup. 'You are clearly from quite a different background. Tell me how you became a saint?'

He looked at her with a hint of a sardonic smile. 'You mock me. I only wanted to help people—people who otherwise had no hope. I lived like them for fourteen years—sleeping on the floor, eating once a day. Sharing my roof with snakes and scorpions.'

'Did your parents influence you?'

His reply was stark, the black eyes flashing. 'No!' He did not elaborate, but picked up the cup with nervous energy and drank again with elegance.

'Was it surgery you did?' asked Hannah.

'Yes—everything that turned up, from Caesarians to cataracts—whatever was needed. Often acting as my own anaesthetist. You cannot know how rewarding it was. No one can. No one here.'

Hannah tried again to get at the man behind the anger. 'Dr Riviero, do you think there are no worthy people on Gran Canaria? Do all poor people have to be virtuous? Is everyone in India wonderful?'

She received for her trouble a withering look from those midnight eyes. 'That is a foolish question. It is just that out there my heart was at peace every night, because I give something to people who expect nothing.'

She nodded, getting used to his scorn. 'Instead of charging overfed tourists for aspirins and antacids?'

He was irritatingly superior. 'Someone has to do it. Not I, if I get well.'

'That's fortunate for Canaria. Who'd want you around, preaching and glowering at people who try to be pleasant to you!' She stood to move the tea tray with a flurry of skirt and petticoat. When she came back she didn't sit down, but stood at the edge of the verandah, looking out at the holidaymakers on the beach, listening to their cheerful cries. Ramón Riviero said nothing, but Hannah suddenly sensed that he was near. She felt the warmth of his body before her arms were gripped. She felt the actual contact of the length of him, that she had been trying not to look at. In a whisper he said, 'My words hurt you a little, *no*?'

She didn't turn, didn't move, although her whole body was alive now, responding to vital overtures that were felt rather than spoken. She tried very hard to keep her voice steady. 'I suppose you're proud of that? You may be a god in India, but here you have a lot to learn about manners, Dr Riviero.'

He let go her arms, but did not move away from her,

their bodies parallel. 'I do not need friends—the world is my friend. I am appalled at the complacency of people here. I still wonder at the miracle of being able to eat every day. May God keep me from ever showing greed! I do not need friends—not here.'

'Everybody needs friends. I've never before met anyone so arrogant that they thought they didn't. Are you so perfect, then, that you can stand alone?'

In the silence between them the waves slashed at the grey sand, and the bathers laughed and whooped. Hannah stood at the edge of the verandah, where the bougainvillea was trying to flourish in the dry soil, to curl up one of the posts. Ramón Riviero stood behind her, and the warmth of his body was almost painful as she recognised her desire to turn to him. His voice now was just a murmur in her consciousness. 'I was wrong earlier. I do not hate you, Hannah Day, only my own feebleness.'

She knew she must take charge of this situation before he did. In spite of his illness he was not a weakling. She took a deep breath, and swung round . . . only to find his arms already around her, locked as though that was the only place for them to be. She said firmly, 'You know I can't fight you. And I'm probably too proud to scream.'

'I believe so. Do you want to scream? I do have a physical advantage.' His face was very close to hers. And the way he said the word 'physical' in that devastating accent made her body want to melt into his. Ramón Riviero clearly knew women. He gently brought her completely within the circle of his arms, very close against him, then bent and brushed her lips with his, lightly as a humming bird, and Hannah was defenceless. She allowed his kiss, loved it, unable to move away. His body was sweet against hers, his mouth hard and expert and mobile. From his easy arousal she knew that it was a long time since he had taken a woman. She couldn't blame him for the kiss; she blamed herself. She ought to have known that her simple dress, bare feet and loose hair would be provoking to a man such as this. She knew how he hungered for her at that moment, but she also recognised that it was a basic hunger. It was not Hannah

Day he wanted, but any woman. That thought made her strong to pull away.

She had lost her innocence at university. It had not been unpleasant, but she hadn't cared much for the boy; they had only drunk too much wine. She had resolved then that she would never allow herself to get into a situation she couldn't control. She moved away from his grasp, trying to keep her tone cool, although her breathing was laboured. 'You've got your own back now, for the shame of having to ask a woman for a job. You've proved you're stronger. Do you feel better now?'

'Come back, Hannah.' His voice was thick, his eyes commanding. He was very handsome, and it was impossible not to feel his need, his desperate longing. Hannah began to fear him—not because of his strength, but because she knew his eyes were hypnotising her. 'You want to come, don't you?' His broken English both enchanted and terrified her.

She looked into his eyes, accepting the challenge of his commanding ego. 'Yes,' she answered truthfully. 'But I won't. And you must go now.'

'Rubbish.' He did not let go of her gaze, though he was not touching her physically. She was captured by his eyes that were willing her to move back to his arms, to accept the inevitability of his passion, his human need and hers.

'Ramón, please go. And if you have any sense, don't come back to San Agustín.'

He gave a short laugh. The spell was broken then, but neither of them moved away, still close enough to feel each other's breath. 'You think you can command me, *mujer*? You are nothing better than a tourist yourself, making money out of these pathetic creatures who fill the hotels and the bars and drink cheap *cerveza* every night until they vomit? I was born in San Agustín. I belong here—appalling though I find it now. No foreign female will tell Riviero when to leave.'

Hannah retorted as proudly as he, 'I can't force you to leave. But this hospital is mine. I paid for it, and I run it. I take on whom I like. And I tell you, Ramón Riviero, you will never enter it again.'

He looked down at her with arrogance, then he sauntered away, leaning with one arm against a post looking out at sea. 'My father could buy this place a hundred times over. He only has to say the word and the local council will have you out. Not that he will—I have taken pity on you, Hannah Day. You are a loser. There is no challenge in you.'

She sensed that his words were born out of resentment that she had found him resistable. She felt a surge of power. Flinging back her hair, she said softly, 'You don't want me now? Truly, Riviero? Are you a good *catolico*? Swear that you don't want me.' She mocked him now, aware of her own ability to attract, and of his hunger. It was a dangerous game to play, but he had aroused something in her that enjoyed the danger. 'Look at me, Riviero.'

He turned and looked at her, his voice low now, menacing as the growl of a panther. 'So you wish to prove how cheap you are?'

The blood throbbed in Hannah's ears as she tried to control her anger and excitement. They seemed able to rile each other to the point of violence. She said, 'Yes, show me! And then go away from here and let me see if you're proud of yourself.'

His jaw tightened at that and she saw his fingers grip into fists. And she knew she had won. He would not make love to her now. In spite of his animal hunger, he had something in him that would not treat her as an object. She could almost have fallen in love with him at that moment, but all she wanted now was for him to leave and never come here again.

The breakers roared and lashed at the grey sand. Hannah stood, outwardly calm, inwardly coping with a hurricane. Looking down at her own hands, which were clasped together so that the nails bit into the flesh, she said in as normal a voice as possible, 'You're too clever for this place. Even if you took the place, I'd know how you despise me, the place, the tourists . . .'

He faced her. It was strange that their faces had not altered, to register the emotional trauma each had subjected each other to. She found that she could look into his eyes now, and he in hers, without the overwhelming feeling of possession. He said quietly, 'I could do the job and hide the scorn. I'm enough of a professional for that.'

'I know. But you can't possibly still want to stay. Why?'

A look of pain crossed his face. 'Pablo thinks I have more chance of getting over my illness in the climate where I was born.'

'And your father? If he's rich, why not stay with him?'

'I dislike him. He is a miser, and I would not ask him for a peseta. His money is for himself alone. I had to plead and cry and shout to be allowed to study medicine. He spent every holiday telling me how selfish I was not to go into his business.'

Hannah understood him better now. 'So even now he's not proud of what you are? What you have done?'

For the first time, Ramón showed weakness, and reached for the chair to sit down. Hannah sat opposite to him, to make him feel less conspicuous. The tremulous beating of her heart was now almost normal again. He spoke quietly, his accent increasingly attractive when his voice posed no threat. 'No. Why should he admire me? I have made no money—that is his criterion of success.' He looked out to sea, seeing only his own memories. 'When I had spent a particularly bad day in India, when I had saved many lives, exhausted myself—then I was happy because I felt I had somehow expiated his sin of greed, by using his money that made me into a doctor.'

She looked with pity at his thin face. 'He drove you to it, then. He's made you so ill—your own father.'

His mocking smile came back briefly. 'You are over-dramatic.'

'I'm a lot of things you disapprove of,' she smiled, and was ridiculously pleased when he smiled back, the dark eyes for a moment readable. 'You——' but their conversation was interrupted by an urgent banging on the door.

'*Medico! Medico!*'

Hannah stood up. 'I must go.'

'I'll come.' He didn't ask permission, merely followed her as she pulled on her white coat, stethoscope in one pocket, sphygmomanometer in the other, thermometer and pen in the top one. A man stood in the waiting room, banging on the desk. 'My daughter, doctor—she's fainted, on the beach. It happened yesterday as well, but I thought it was the heat. She looked bad, doctor.'

'She's down there?'

'Yes. My wife is with her.'

'Show me.' Hannah had forgotten Ramón. She grabbed her emergency bag and ran down the beach path with the man. A girl about fifteen lay on a towel, her face pallid under her tan, the forehead streaked with damp hair. Hannah was on her knees at once, checking pulse, blood pressure, temperature. The girl opened her eyes and moaned, then vomited a little on the tissue her mother held for her. Hannah asked, 'Has she had any injury?'

The mother answered. 'No, doctor, but she was like this before her operation—tummy pains all night. I was up with her. We thought it was the food.'

Hannah examined the abdomen, easy because the girl wore a bikini. 'I see a new appendix scar. How long ago?'

'Two months.'

'Did she make a good recovery?'

'At first she was fine, but she's never been as chirpy as she used to be.'

Hannah completed her examination. 'It seems to me that she's developed some post-operative infection—subphrenic abscess.' She gently palpated the area just under the diaphragm. The girl opened her eyes again and cried out weakly. Hannah said, 'Yes, the trouble is here. She'll have to go to Las Palmas for operation.'

A man's voice intervened. Hannah had forgotten Ramón was still there. He was examining the diaphragm area. 'I'll do it, Hannah. You have the facilities—I saw your theatre.'

She looked across the recumbent patient. 'The theatre is functional, yes. Are you sure?'

'Yes. I agree with you about the subphrenic abscess—and I also think the operation should be as soon as possible.'

'I'll call the nurses.' Hannah turned to the father. 'Go and ring that bell.' He obeyed, clanging the bell in the hospital porch to alert the two nurses and Esteban the driver, who were always within hearing distance.

Carla and Rosita were at the hospital before Ramón and Hannah got the patient back. She told them to prepare theatre for surgery. Ramón was already scrubbing up in the tiny anteroom. Rosita, masked and gowned, laid out his gown, mask and gloves. They acted together without rush, as though they had been a team for years. Carla prepared the patient, and stayed with her. 'You are a very lucky girl, to have a top-class surgeon on the spot like this.' Carla was still impressed, the name Riviero being famous locally.

The girl really was quite ill. As Hannah donned her own gown, she knew Ramón was right; the forty-minute drive to Las Palmas might have proved fatal if the abscess had burst. She placed the halothane in position, and filled the syringe with pentathol.

'You are qualified?' Ramón was at her side, only his handsome eyes visible, the unruly black hair hidden by the cap.

'Yes, don't worry. I've done anaesthetics, acupuncture, homeopathy and advanced obstetrics.'

'Anaesthetics will do for now.' He wriggled his fingers into the gloves held for him by Rosita. 'Shall we get started?'

He incised deftly, quickly, and Rosita mopped at the blood as he opened the peritoneum. The abscess was grossly swollen and unhealthy-looking. From her place at the patient's head, Hannah could see that illness had not blunted Ramón's skill. Neatly, with intense patience, he removed the offending tissue, without making a single clumsy or unnecessary move. Hannah's admiration mounted.

'We have local antibiotics?' He looked up. Hannah had already placed them ready at Rosita's elbow. She met the black eyes, and they held hers for a moment in mutual appreciation. 'I see the hospital at San Agustín has a most competent doctor.' He reached for the stitches now, and put in seven neat sutures, knotted with practised dexterity. Hannah watched his fingers, fascinated.

Later the two doctors disrobed, and when the patient was resting back in the small ward, they sat together on the verandah. Hannah felt as though she had known Ramón for years. Not that she liked him, or wanted him here permanently, but as they exchanged a smile of relief and thanks, she hoped that perhaps they might meet again occasionally . . .

Rosita came out. 'Who will speak to the parents?' she asked. She had taken off her theatre clothes, and her lovely shining hair and voluptuous figure were shown to advantage by the neat white overall. Then she gave a gasp. 'Ramón, it is you! You have come back. I thought you were dead.' She spoke in Spanish.

'Rosita Alfonso—I never thought I would see you again.' His face was openly smiling, his words sounding like a caress in his native tongue, as he stood up and went over to her, his tiredness forgotten. Their conversation became low, inaudible. He didn't touch her, but from the way her eyes shone as she gazed up at him, it was plain they were special to each other.

Hannah went to the door. 'I'll see the parents,' she said, but nobody was listening. She went and chatted to the worried parents, allowed them to sit by the bed for a while.

When she returned to the verandah they were still talking, seated now and looking into each other's faces. Rosita was saying, 'You've been to the Villa?'

'Not yet. I am not ready.'

'You must, Ramón. It is not right that you are here and do not see Papa.'

'I will go soon,' he promised.

'And you are really going to work here?'

'I do not know.'

'This is not good enough for you, Ramón.'

'I will explain why I am here. But tell me—your father and brothers, they are well? And your old uncle?'

'They are well. But they still must fight, Ramón.'

Carla came out with a tray of coffee. She handed a cup

to Hannah. The others didn't even notice her. Carla smiled indulgently. 'So this is Rosita's secret! I knew she must have a secret lover.'

'You think . . . ?' Hannah found she couldn't say the words.

'I think so. Just look at them.' Carla seemed delighted to have found out Rosita's secret. 'Hey, coffee here!' They turned and smiled, so handsome and well matched physically, sitting so close together. They still had not touched, yet the intimacy was there, the regard, the obvious delight in their murmured Spanish reunion.

Hannah drank her coffee hurriedly, burning her throat and tongue. She made an excuse about tidying the theatre; she could not bear to sit still any longer. Then she went back to the front door and gazed out at the stony path to the road, the busy Las Palmas highway, the Alfa-Sud like a black beast lurking in the scrub. The cement lorries were bringing their last loads before the end of the day, grinding up the hill in third gear, belching out diesel fumes as they climbed. For the first time she noticed the name painted on the lorry doors: 'Riviero Cement Factory, San Agustín.' So that was how Ramón's father had become rich—a developing tourist industry, a sharp-eyed entrepreneur who realised how much cement would be needed for all the apartments and hotels along the beaches. How ironic, that Ramón should hate the very tourists who had helped his father to make the money that had turned his son into a doctor.

She looked down at her feet, where her strawberries still lay, scattered, ruined . . . In this one afternoon there seemed to have been some sort of volcanic eruption in Hannah Day's life. Ah well, it was over now. As the sun dipped low, she felt calmer. Soon he would leave. She knew she could not have him back. She could not stand the trauma of having this man in her life for another day.

She heard the phone ring in the hall, and went in to take it. Carla had already lifted the receiver. 'It is Dr Rodriguez,' she told Hannah.

'Hello, Pablo.'

'I have sent you an assistant—sorry I did not let you

know in advance. He has arrived?'

'Pablo, how could you! How could you ever think a self-opinionated top surgeon would fit into my little hospital? It's the most ludicrous idea you've ever had!'

'Hannah, my angel, don't say that. Let me explain. He needs a job. He's been seriously ill, and I'm very fond of him. He needs a few months of light duties in his own homeland. We've been close since college days, and he means a lot to me—and to Dolores.'

Hannah paused, her heart sinking. 'I think you mean I must take him.'

'Would it be so very dreadful—to help a colleague in trouble? When the busy season is coming?'

She sighed. 'It isn't going to be easy.' She could hear Rosita's laugh.

It was Pablo's turn to pause. 'He's a good man, angel—the best.'

'So he told me.' Her tone was ironic. 'We aren't —awfully friendly just now.'

'I see.' Pablo's voice echoed his disappointment. 'Oh well, it was just an idea. I thought you'd be so good for him, being calm and tolerant and kind . . .'

Hannah interrupted. 'Stop, Pablo! I can't bear his sob-story any longer—or your crawling flattery. The job is his, I give you my word.'

'God bless you! I'm very grateful.'

'I only hope I know what I'm doing,' she sighed. 'He'll probably walk out anyway.'

She stood for a long time by the phone in the growing darkness, her hand still on the receiver. She did want an assistant—but this assistant?

It was very quiet. She walked slowly out at the back of the hospital. The lights were going on in the beach cafés and bars. Ramón Riviero was sitting alone. Hannah stood for a moment, looking down at the back of his hair, the set of the noble head on broad shoulders, the yearning look as he stared out to sea, at the endless rolling billows. He seemed to sense her presence, and turned round in his chair. 'Hannah. You will wish me to go now.' He smiled. 'There is no charge for the surgery—I needed the practice.' He stood up. 'I will be on my way if you wish.'

'No.'

He let out a gentle sigh, and she saw something come to life in his eyes, very dark now in the failing light. She had done something good, but would it be good for her, to have Ramón Riviero around every day . . . Ramón and his ravishing Rosita . . . ? *'Gracias, muchas gracias.'*

She only noticed then how weary he looked. And how politely he had thanked her, after his rudeness earlier on. His eyes, still masterful, were ringed with black. She felt a rush of compassion. 'You should get some rest, Ramón. You want a room here?'

'I do not wish to be an irritant to you. I will stay at Rosita's mother's house. She is an old friend—all her family work for my father. Rosita says she will be cooking *mero* for me tonight. She remembered how we used to enjoy it as children . . .' There was a silence, then Ramón said as though talking to himself, 'I have watched the Indian vultures circling round the corpses in the evenings . . . and the glow in the sky has reminded me of San Agustín, and sitting on the harbour wall with my school friends . . .'

Hannah recognised the stirrings of sexual jealousy within her. She must not allow it to affect her. 'OK, then, Rosita's mother's it is.'

He said quietly, 'Hannah, sit for a moment.' She sat opposite to him, not as close as Rosita had done. 'You forgive my manners, then? I have some great resentment at the world sometimes. I cannot explain—but I do not mean to be hurtful.'

His voice played on her emotions, stirring her immediately to tenderness. She squashed the feelings promptly. Briskly she said, 'Well now, how about being on call for me tonight? After your *mero*, of course. I have a date in Puerto de Mogan.'

'Very well, I will come. What time?'

She hated herself for asking him. He was tired and ill. But she was committed now. 'Seven-thirty?'

Ramón walked off down the steps, not bothering to take his jacket she had rescued from the dust. She watched his slim, lithe figure as it merged into the general holidaymakers down at the beach. She sat, immobile, not exactly thinking, but allowing the experiences of the day to wash over her again and again. She had never met anyone like Ramón Riviero. If she had any sense she would make sure he went out of her life. But Pablo and Dolores were good friends, and she would be churlish to refuse this, their first request for a favour.

She saw his tall figure returning, and looked at her watch. It was seven-thirty, and she had not moved, had not eaten. Hastily she ran inside and changed her dress to an orange silk, pretending she was in a hurry. Ramón climbed the stairs with Rosita Alfonso, and Hannah gave them a brilliant smile. 'Thanks so much for coming. I should be back before midnight.' And before they could ask her any questions, she had backed out her little Spanish jeep. Ramón and Rosita were walking among the stunted palms at the edge of the beach. The sun was very low now, sending their long shadows almost to the hospital steps. Their heads were very close together, their faces animated.

Hannah stamped on the accelerator, swerved round in a cloud of dust, and drove at top speed along the winding cliff road to Mogan, half an hour away in the opposite direction from Las Palmas. She had no date, no friend in Mogan, just a desperate need to get away from the hospital that night. Too much had happened; too much might happen that she was not prepared for. She must be clear-sighted about the future now. She bought a smoked fish and a papaya from the village and took them back to the car to eat, looking out across the small pretty harbour.

The fishing boats had all gone out, their little lights twinkling. She had watched each one, envying the feeling of freedom as they left the shelter of the harbour and made for the open sea.

It was midnight when she got back, trying not to make a noise as she parked the jeep. She went up the front steps, taking out her key. The strawberries still lay in the dust, as she picked her way through them in the moonlight.

CHAPTER TWO

THE MORNING was fresh and young, the sun just appearing through the mist of the mountains in the centre of the island. Hannah walked down to the water, barefooted as usual in the grey sand. She pulled off her cotton wrap and left it in a heap over a rock, while she braced her body in the mild early sun to run into the icy breakers. The first shock made her gasp and splutter, but she swam out strongly, reaching calmer water. She had spent a sad and pointless evening last night, staring out over the harbour wall. She was angry with herself for behaving so childishly, yet she knew she had to.

Why? Had it been so very important to show her unwelcome new partner her independence? Hannah had thought so last night. This crazy surgeon might be with her for some months—though she doubted whether either of them could stand so much. But he must never get an inkling of the physical power he wielded over her. It would have been easy to allow her attraction to him to show. But how fatal for her heart, so easily broken. How fatal for her self-esteem, for the very future of her hospital at San Agustín, where up to now she had been perfectly contented. How lucky that she had recognised the danger in time to do something about it.

She swam well, vigorously, glad of the health that allowed her to exert herself like this, in spite of an almost sleepless night. That 'friend in Mogan' would be needed again, she knew. She would need him, to get away from the powerful personality of Ramón Riviero, who had walked into her life and taken away her peace. She could not be jealous of Rosita—Rosita, who was his physical equal, who came to life so obviously when he came into a room. If they suited each other, it must be nothing to Hannah . . . She had told him herself that one did not have to like one's colleagues, so long as they were efficient.

She walked back up the beach, her wrap carelessly over her shoulder. There was no one about so early to see her slim body in its small black bikini. The grey sand caked blackly on her wet feet, but it would soon brush away. She felt invigorated. But she still sighed, knowing that a serpent had entered her own private little Eden. Two sharp black eyes, deep as midnight, had usurped her place as master of her own destiny. She couldn't allow it.

'*Buenos dias.*'

She looked up in surprise, though she could not but know whose voice it was. He was sitting on the verandah, in her favourite chair. His eyes were narrowed against the sparkle of the sun on the water. Two glasses of fresh lemon juice stood on the table at his side. 'I bring you some juice after your swim.'

'Thank you.' Hannah hoped he wasn't going to be nice. She preferred him prickly—it kept a distance between them.

'You will sit?'

She was still standing up, and she pulled the wrap around her suddenly before she sat down. The sun was already warmer, beginning to dry her damp hair. She wondered if Ramón had spent the night with Rosita . . . It was a thought that wouldn't go away. He was so very masculine; where else would he sleep?

'I have something else for you,' he told her.

'There's no need to be nice, you know.'

'I know,' he said gently, and pushed a small square package into her hands. 'It did not cost much.' His eyes held a hint of a smile.

Hannah pulled off the brown paper wrapper. Inside was a basket of perfect red strawberries. She couldn't help saying, 'How beautiful!'

'They are from my father's plantation. Rosita's brother brings a van down from San Nicolás every morning for the market. And you did lose all your berries yesterday because of me.'

'It didn't matter.' Her heart lifted at his thoughtfulness. And then, foolishly, she felt her lips tremble. Tears

started in her eyes. She had never been easily touched
. . . but somehow, being half in love with someone
against your will made you different from the person
you thought you were. She was discovering things
about herself that she didn't know. A little scared, she
swallowed, and hoped he would not notice her glistening
eyes, as her drying hair fell about her face.

'What time do you want me to be on duty?' asked
Ramón.

Thankful to get down to business, Hannah reeled off
the daily routine. 'There's no need for us both to be
here. We must make out a rota. Dr. Arora in the town
square always does Wednesday, so we'll keep that free
for both of us. But it will be less strain, not being on call
twenty-four hours a day. I—I—well, I'm grateful to
have some help . . .'

'Pablo told me. He was worried about you—he said
you were too conscientious.'

'He was worried about you too,' she smiled.

His dark face was impossibly attractive as he met her
look. 'Shall I tell Pablo to stop worrying?'

'Not yet.'

'What's the problem?' he asked.

'We—don't like each other very much.' Hannah's
light tone showed him she was only bantering with him.
Yet there was a grain of truth there too.

'OK. But I am efficient, no? You told me yesterday
that colleagues do not have to like each other.'

He was being easily friendly now, and that could be
very frightening. It could become all too simple to allow
her mask to drop, to let him see her simple affection,
already growing as they spoke. She said briefly,
'Right—then we'll settle for efficiency. And the fact that
you suffer from this incurable superiority complex.'

'I am making a very big effort to control it.' There was
sardonic amusement on his face. 'This is a big leap for
me. I am not used to idleness and fun all around me. In
India there was very little of that.'

She said firmly, 'You'd better not make comparisons,
or you'll become permanently angry. You must already
feel irritated at the way I go out and swim just like the

tourists. You must be wondering how God can make it possible for this to happen on the same planet as all the suffering you've seen.'

Ramón nodded several times. Then he picked up his glass and drank deeply. 'Yes, you are right,' he answered slowly. 'I must be badly made, Hannah. I cannot adjust yet to what I am, to what life has made of me—a useless hulk. I have to get angry, I have to cry to heaven for putting me down just here, when I want, I need so much to be there.'

'Thanks for saying it. But don't forget it isn't easy for the rest of us if you keep showing it.' Hannah smoothed her hair back with the towel. There was silence on the verandah, with only the rolling waves and the shrill cry of seabirds overhead.

He said suddenly, 'You saw your friend last night?'

For a moment she wondered what he meant. Then she recollected her 'friend'. 'My friend is Mogan? Yes. Yes, I did.'

'He has a boat?'

Hannah said primly, 'What makes you think it's a man?'

'You went very quickly, as though impatient. Anyway, a woman alone is a sad sight.' He shrugged. 'For your sake I hope it is a man.'

'That's . . .' Hannah controlled her sudden outburst and said in quieter tones, 'That's both patronising and sexist.'

'Probably,' he shrugged.

'We must both make the effort to accept each other for what we are. You are patronising, superior and sexist; I am pleasure-seeking and shallow. A little courtesy and tolerance is obviously needed from both of us.'

'Thank you for the lesson. Funny how my faults seem less than yours.'

Hannah looked across. He seemed to be serious. The sun was getting warmer, the day livelier, with tourists coming out, and stallholders opening shutters. She said quietly, 'I'm not sure how long my fuse is. But I warn you, I can probably do more damage than you think from my small size.' She was only half joking; her blood was beginning to seethe. Why, oh, why was he still so attractive to her, when she ought to dislike the very ground he trod, the way he had just spoken to her? Violence snapped at her heels, excitement—even danger—as it had yesterday. She stood up suddenly, collected her towel and turned to go in.

'Hannah?'

She turned. Ramón was standing now, almost a foot taller than she was, his broad shoulders blocking out the low sun. She looked up into those compelling eyes, and for a moment everything else vanished. Then he said quietly, his voice in her ears tender yet rough, musical yet harsh, jangling on her feelings, 'Thank you—for putting up with me. I had to be here, you know.'

They stood together, a couple in the sun. From a distance they were close and intimate, looking into each other's faces with a closeness of lovers. But for Hannah came the vision of the comely Rosita, which helped her turn away from the striking figure before her as though she couldn't care less. She said calmly, 'I do see that.' She walked straight inside, into the shower, and turned the jet full on. She stood under it for a long time, trying with the stinging cold drops to erase the thought of Rosita. But it refused to go. And she knew she must work with the image of them together still before her.

She scrubbed herself dry, harder than necessary, and towelled her hair briskly. Instead of a comfortable dress, she put on a slim-fitting grey skirt and a short-sleeved white blouse with a small black bow at the neck. She tied her hair back with a narrow velvet ribbon, and brought out her reading glasses. The annoying part of all this was that she knew she was deliberately emphasising the efficient side of her nature and smothering the poetic. But it did seem terribly important to her self-respect at that moment to show she was not trying to look sexually appealing.

She heard Rosita's laugh before she saw them together. When she entered the consulting room, they were both there, the whispered Spanish chatter punctuated with giggles. It angered her, even though she had promised herself it would not. Fortunately there were several patients waiting, and she was able to turn her mind away from her staff. She did mention to Carla that some people weren't doing anything useful, but she was annoyed with herself for saying it. It didn't matter; she had to learn to live with Ramón's sexual activity.

Carla said, 'Dr Riviero is only being pleasant. He is such a gentleman.'

'You like him around, don't you?'

Carla laughed. 'What do you think? I'm only human.'

Oh yes, Carla, how terribly, hurtfully true. Hannah smiled—she hoped with spontaneity. 'I'm glad you're content,' she said.

'Dr Hannah, don't tell me you're immune? Don't you find him handsome?'

Hannah froze at the suggestion. She hated herself for being jealous of Rosita's happiness. She wrote her patient's notes with a determined scribble. 'Send me the next!' she ordered.

'No need to shout!' Carla looked hurt.

Hannah didn't apologise. But she was dissatisfied with her work that morning. She handed out diarrhoea sachets, headache pills, and cream for sunburn and insect stings. And she wondered if Ramón was right to despise what she did, calling it worthless medicine.

The door was pushed open. She thought it was Carla with another patient, but the voice was masculine, the one that had echoed in her brain all morning. 'Hannah, do you know it is after one?'

She looked up at Ramón. He had spent the morning at the beach, and his arms were browner than yesterday. His shirt was unbuttoned at the front, showing an expensive gold chain over the black hairs there. She turned her eyes hurriedly from his figure. 'I do have a watch,' she told him.

'You should eat something. With my illness, I know all too well you should always watch your blood sugar level.'

Hannah snapped without meaning to. 'One minute you make me feel guilty for being able to afford to eat, the next, you shout at me for not eating. My poor conscience can't take much more of you!'

He said in a low voice, 'Take a break, Hannah. While you're away, I'll work out a rota, as we agreed—one that keeps us apart, seeing that we irritate each other so much.'

She regretted shouting, but could not bring herself to apologise. 'All right, go ahead. You can put Carla on with me.'

'Why?'

She turned to face him. Was he seriously saying he didn't know? 'Why not? I can see you and Rosita are—old friends. It will be nicer for you to work with someone you like.'

'That's very thoughtful of you, Hannah.' His voice was neutral; he might have been laughing at her. She didn't know any more.

She said under her breath, but so that he could hear, 'If you're going to see patients in here, would you please either wear a white coat or button your shirt? You look like a gigolo.'

She didn't wait for his reply, though she thought she had caused some response, and was perversely glad. She went through to the kitchen, where Esteban was sitting with his feet on another chair, eating grapes. Hannah smiled, her mental tension winding down. Esteban was familiar. He was good-looking, innocent at twenty-six, with a large black moustache and a great love of cars, and of eating and drinking. 'Still eating?' She took a couple of his grapes.

Esteban stood up, with natural good manners. 'Not had lunch yet.'

She smiled. 'I'm going to Pepe's. Coming? On me?'

He followed her, friendly but not pushy. As they walked the few yards down the beach path, Hannah noticed that some girls at one of the stalls were watching them covertly from behind a large stand of sun-tan lotion and cotton hats. She said casually, 'You have a girl-friend, Esteban?'

He grinned, noticing them too. 'Those girls—they always tease me. They all say they wish to go out with Esteban, but they are silly. I do not like the girls much.'

He paused, and went on, 'There is one who likes me very much, I think.' His gentle eyes showed modesty.

'Am I allowed to know who?' smiled Hannah.

'Maria Moreno. She works at the boutique down there, opposite the Pirates' Cave Bar.' Esteban looked down at Hannah, who was dwarfed by his muscular frame. 'She is nice, but *mucho timida*.' He grinned again. 'Sometimes I think I like boys more than girls!'

Hannah's heart sank. Did even her nice steady faithful Esteban have problems, then? Boys better than girls? 'Why, Esteban? Why boys?' she asked.

'That is easy. They like better things—they like motorbikes and cars and engines, no? Girls, they talk of silly things. Cars they do not like.'

Very relieved, Hannah agreed with him. 'Girls don't often understand how cars work, you see.' An idea began to form in her mind. 'You understand cars very well, Esteban, I've noticed.' Indeed, they never had to take the van they had converted to an ambulance to be mended at a garage; Esteban always serviced it himself.

'There is nothing I do not know about an engine—any engine.' He wasn't boasting—just stating a fact.

They reached Pepes, and took their usual places on the tall stools at the bar. Pepe waved a laconic wrist and set their usual Sangria before them without being asked. 'You got a new *medico*?' he queried.

'You don't miss much, Pepe,' laughed Hannah.

'Nice-looking guy. Good choice, Dr Hannah.'

'Not my choice, I'm afraid. He's from round here, and wanted to come back.'

The bar-owner's thin face became alert. He came over and hissed, 'It is Riviero?'

Surprised by his secretive posture, Hannah nodded. 'Riviero.'

His face brightened. 'Thank God! This man we need.' And he went back to his work.

She looked at him for a moment, then dismissed his remark as meaning nothing. He brought them paella, but said no more about Ramón—almost like a conspirator who didn't want to give himself away. Hannah was faintly troubled. Pepe was no fool. But she knew he was into politics, and refrained from drawing him out further. He had to be careful, in order to keep his business. But the rumour was he was a Communist in his spare time. As he had so little spare time, it was not regarded as serious.

Hannah turned back to the germ of her idea. 'Esteban, do you know that big garage in Mogan?'

'*Muy bien.* I know the owner and all the mechanics.' His face brightened at the choice of subject to talk about. 'You want a car from there, Dr Hannah? *Muy bien* place. You need a car—a jeep is not good enough for a medico, huh?'

'How do you mean?'

'A *medico* should always have the Mercedes, yes? If a humble taximan can have a Mercedes, then we must . . .'

'Hold on, Esteban!' laughed Hannah. 'I don't want a big diesel monster—there are enough fumes in San Agustín already. But a car—yes, I am thinking about it.'

Esteban began to list the makes of cars his garage-owner friend stocked. 'He will not cheat you, *lo prometo.*' Hannah liked the idea more and more. She had toyed with the idea for several months. Now that she had discovered a garage in Mogan itself—it would give her a reason to get out of Ramón's way without having to pretend. She would have a genuine friend in Mogan. She would go and test-drive all the cars he had, instead of sitting morosely at the wheel of her jeep, watching the fishermen and the seagulls, as she had that first night.

Pleased with her decision at lunch, she left Esteban eyeing the little girl at the boutique. At her age Hannah had been grappling with A-level Physics. She walked past the gift shops and bars, the fat ladies in bikinis and the racks of hats reading 'I love Canaria'. She hardly noticed them now, except to smile and greet the proprietors by name. Ramón Riviero disliked tourists. He could not appreciate the spirit of comradeship there was down at the beach community. There wasn't really a place for an idealist in San Agustín.

Hannah paused with a sharp intake of breath as she reached the hospital. Ramón was standing against the

verandah post, looking rather like a cowboy, hands in
pockets, the lock of hair over one eye. He was talking
earnestly to three men—local men in jeans and rather
ragged shirts. One was gesticulating, then thumping his
fist on his palm to make a point. Ramón stood, cool and
unmoving, rapping out occasional retorts, his face unreadable. He looked up suddenly, and saw Hannah.
'*Vamos!*' he said to them quietly. The men had melted
into the surroundings by the time Hannah had climbed
the steps to the verandah.

'Who was that?' she asked him.

'They are just workmen I used to know.'

He wasn't saying. She asked, 'Any calls?'

'Yes, the Verona Hotel rang. Some lady is sick. You
want me to go?'

'No, Riviero. How could I ask you to visit some fat
tourist who's eaten too much?' Her voice was scornful.
'How long ago did they ring?'

'Only two minutes. And I will go if you wish. You are
the boss.'

She felt his pain, at having to admit it—to be sub-
servient to a woman looking after minor ailments, after
his brilliant career in India. She felt it too. She said more
gently, 'We're partners. But I'll go.'

She went in past his tall lean figure. He made no move
to step back, so she had to brush against him as she went
in, felt the hairs on his bare brown arm, the strong hard
muscles. He murmured as she touched and passed him,
'Button your blouse, woman. You look like a tart!'

Striding swiftly indoors, appalled, Hannah clenched
her fists and looked down. The top three buttonholes of
her blouse were a bit too big, and the buttons had come
out. She stamped her foot irritably as she refastened
them and went to get her emergency bag from the
consulting room. Trust Ramón not to miss the chance of
humiliating her! At least he had done it in private. But
his words rankled.

She went out the back way. It wasn't necessary, she
could reach her jeep better from the front door, but she
wanted to have a final dig at her annoying partner.

'Why don't you run along to Rosita's house and have a

lie down?' And she started the engine before he had time to reply. She ought not to have said that. She was ashamed of herself before she got to the end of the drive. But he was an arrogant bastard, to speak to her like that. She tugged again at her buttons as she swung out into the main road. She must learn to grow a thicker skin, if Ramón was going to be around the full year she had agreed to.

The patient in the hotel room was neither fat nor rich. She hadn't been drinking or eating too much. The poor creature was having a heart attack. Her husband sat by her bed as she clutched at her chest, her face clammy and her hands cold in the heat of the room. Hannah went straight to the phone to call Esteban. Ramón took the phone, and it was as though their feud had never happened. When a patient was involved, they worked together like an efficient machine, for the good of the patient. Ramón said, 'Yes, he's here. Is there oxygen in the van?'

'There should be. Would you check, please? I'll get on to Las Palmas right away to expect her.'

'Right.'

Mr Greaves, the husband, said glumly, holding his wife's hand as Hannah gave her an injection for the pain, 'This was our first holiday since our last boy finished college. We could never afford to go away before.' There were tears in his eyes.

'Try not to worry,' said Hannah gently. 'We'll get her to intensive care within half an hour.'

'But a heart attack—that's serious, isn't it, doctor?'

'Sometimes. Tests will show. But I feel this isn't too bad—she'll pull through. You can come with us in the van.'

Esteban stepped on the gas, in a way he fully enjoyed when permitted. Hannah sat beside Mrs Greaves, monitoring her blood pressure, and thinking how narrow-minded of Ramón to despise people like the Greaves, who had spent their lifetime until now devoted to their family. Didn't they deserve a holiday in the sun? Riviero had tunnel vision where holidaymakers were concerned . . . Hannah pulled herself together as the patient gripped her hand. She must get Ramón Riviero out of her system.

Hannah waited in the hospital corridor while doctors in the intensive care unit examined Mrs Greaves, keeping up the husband's morale. Just then the Sister came bustling out. 'Hannah! What are you doing here? This lady is your patient?'

It was Dolores Rodriguez, Pablo's wife. 'Yes, Dolores. This is Mr Greaves. We've just brought her here from Puerto Rico.' Hannah watched as the motherly Dolores said all the right things to Mr Greaves. She sent a nurse to bring him a cup of tea, and told him he could see his wife shortly, then she took Hannah to one side. Hannah knew what was coming. 'Dolores, your big heart has overdone it this time. You can't mother Ramón Riviero—it's like trying to cuddle a porcupine!'

'It is Pablo.' The kindly face didn't mind Hannah's protests one bit. 'They are such close friends, Hannah. And Ramón is so good, so idealistic.'

'He's also downright rude most of the time!'

'I'm sure he doesn't mean it.' Dolores' face showed genuine affection.

Hannah took a deep breath. 'I took him in like some lonesome waif because I owe you a favour, Dolores. But never ask me to do anything like this again. He shows no gratitude—only scorn. I can't wait until he goes back to his beloved India.'

Dolores' face darkened and she put her hand on Hannah's arm. 'He will never go back. He was found apparently dead, Hannah, lifeless. They were going to put him with the corpses for the vultures. He will never be able to stand it again.'

Hannah felt a twinge of pity at the mental picture. 'Does he know?' she asked.

'Maybe he guesses. Pablo has not told him.'

'That might explain why he's such a pest.'

Dolores patted her arm again. 'Soon you will be friends. You must come to dinner. Wednesday is the day you have off?'

'Yes, but I don't think either of us could stand being

together for a whole evening. We couldn't stay civil that long.'

'Then soon. *Lo antes posible.*'

'*Muy bien. Y muchas gracias.*'

The consultant came out of the ward to speak to them. 'She will recover—the damage to the heart is small,' he told them. They left Mr Greaves with his wife, Dolores with typical generosity promising to give him a lift back to the hotel when she came off duty. Esteban and Hannah went back along the dusty highway at a slower pace.

They picked up Hannah's jeep from the Verona Hotel and she drove down the winding road to the hospital, the sun just setting in an explosion of flame and fire across the emerald ocean. She left the jeep in its usual place and walked slowly down the path and through the hospital, with the cheerful sound of sunbathers going back to hotels and apartments to wash off the grey sand and change for the evening.

Hannah went out to the verandah. The beach was now almost silent, as Pedro folded up the umbrellas and put the sun-loungers straight for the following morning. Two seagulls wheeled across the bay, calling plaintively. The palm trees were stocky and familiar, outlined against the brilliance of the sky. Hannah felt peaceful. San Agustín had its faults, but she never regretted settling here. It suited her. It was home.

Rosita came out. 'How is your patient?' she asked.

'She'll live.' Hannah smiled. Rosita couldn't help being lovely. 'And how is yours?' The girl recovering from the operation was still in the ward.

'She is fine. Ramón has admitted another lady—with pre-eclampsia.'

'Do you want me to see her?' asked Hannah.

'Ramón has done everything—he asked me to tell you.'

'OK, Rosita, thanks. You're staying on duty?'

'Yes, I will stay.'

Hannah went indoors to shower and change. She took a simple dress, and didn't bother with shoes. Raquel, the maid, was sweeping and mopping all the floors before going home. Hannah went out to watch the last of the sunset, carrying a large glass of cold lager. Thank goodness Ramón was off duty; it made the relaxation of the evening all the more complete and sweet. She leaned back, listening to the crashing beauty of the waves. Oh, what bliss, when her irritating lodger wasn't around.

And then she recognised the long strides of a dark silhouette on the beach. He was coming this way! Hannah's heart contracted suddenly, as she remembered what Dolores had told her. Poor man, there was a reason for his intolerance. She must try to be nicer to him. He was climbing the steps now, his eyes on her as he came. The sun had gone now, taking its brilliance with it, but leaving a gentle glow in the clear sky, stretched across them like a turquoise screen of fine silk.

His voice was low and vibrant in the gentle air. 'I guess I have to apologise for what I said before.'

She had forgotten how annoyed she had been when he told her to button her blouse. Now she remembered. 'Please don't bother,' she told him. 'It doesn't suit you to be nice. Just go on being yourself, then we understand one another.'

'You also can be hurtful,' he told her ruefully.

'I wonder where I learned that? I was OK until yesterday.'

He snapped suddenly. 'You are right, *señorita*. Better to stay good enemies than false friends.'

'More honest anyway,' shrugged Hannah.

He came up and sat on the opposite chair. She tried not to look at his face, so tragic and thin, now that she knew how ill he was. Her heart yearned to tell him she understood, but no words came. Ramón turned to her, his voice quiet again. 'You do not see your Mogan friend tonight?'

She had forgotten her Mogan friend. 'Maybe tomorrow.'

'Ah, then you do not love him all that much?'

'You would know, of course, being the expert you are on women.'

He sounded amused. 'I do know women, yes. So?'

'Some women, not all.'

'You think you are different, huh?'

'You don't, obviously,' retorted Hannah. 'So what can I say?'

'You do not wish to talk. Then maybe I will go over to Pepe's.' Pepe the closet Communist. Ramón flung a pebble towards the beach with a gesture of frustration. 'Ah, this stupid liver of mine! I cannot even get drunk to stop the pain in my soul. One beer is my allowance.'

Hannah felt for him then. She knew depression. 'Talk about it, then. You don't think much of me, I know, but I can listen, if it will help.'

Ramón turned half away, and she watched his handsome profile. She could hate his guts, but she couldn't help admiring his looks. The lights were going on all around them. The apartments up the cliffs brightened, one by one. Vivid neon restaurant signs vied with one another in vulgarity. Hannah's heart ached for the pain in the soul of Ramón Riviero, but she dared not say so. He would only say something cutting, hurtful.

'Tell me about India,' she ventured.

She couldn't see his face then, as he stared out to sea, but she knew it was rapt with memories. He sat on the verandah rail and began to talk quietly in his beautiful accent of the terrible beauty and the savage cruelty of life that he had experienced. There was no doubt but that was where he wanted to be. He ached for India. And he must know he would never go back.

He fell silent after a while, his heart too full to speak. Hannah understood, but she could not say so. They both sat in the semi-darkness with their own thoughts. As they sat, a Spanish guitar struck up down in one of the cafés. It was played with dramatic vibrancy that made Hannah's heart quicken. She looked up at Ramón, suddenly excited, sexually stirred by the music. She wanted him then, wanted him badly. But he would despise her for it, and she dared say nothing.

The Iberian passion in that guitar would not let her rest. She sat forward on the chair. 'Shall we go somewhere to eat?' Her voice was low, tentative.

He turned, and she saw he had not been listening. 'What? No, I do not want to eat.'

'Come to the beach café. They have good fish, fresh caught.'

'Miguel's place? You know San Agustín well! I used to go there as a boy.'

Hannah waited, her body taut with longing, as the music floated up to them from the beach. She tried to speak lightly. 'You know what happens if your blood sugar level falls?'

Ramón turned and gave a short laugh. 'Yes, doctor, I know. OK, maybe we will visit Miguel.' He stood up from the rail. 'But there is no need to take me under your wing, you know. I do not need or want that.'

Hannah felt hurt again. 'I'm sorry, I didn't mean . . .'

'Oh, come on, woman! What do you recommend from Miguel's?' His voice was irritable again.

'*Pez espada*. It's very good.'

He laughed again aloud. 'Swordfish? For you? You don't need it, woman. Your tongue is sharp enough already.'

Hannah felt as though he had slapped her face. She got up in a flurry of skirts and rushed indoors. The throbbing of the guitar was fainter there. She bit her lip until she tasted blood, then she ran out to the jeep and started the engine.

CHAPTER THREE

HALFWAY to Mogan, Hannah began to feel better.
Ramón Riviero had not acted out of character. It was
she who had expected more from him than he could be
expected to give. It was she who had reacted to the thrill
of the guitar, felt the sudden emptiness in her life she had
thought to be fulfilled . . . Ramón was no mind-reader;
he couldn't have known how the guitar aroused her.
Hannah began to ridicule herself, flying off like that, like
some teenager in a silly huff. She slowed down along the
cliff highway into Mogan. What on earth was she to do
here? Spend another lonely night sitting by the harbour
wall?

Then her sensible side took over. Now that she had
come this far she might as well eat here. But there would
be no skulking in the car; that was too pathetic for
words—allowing one ill-mannered man to affect her so
profoundly. She didn't realise she could be so very
emotional.

She drove down to the harbour. The village men were
congregated in the tavern near the boatyard, drinking
wine and gambling in the lighted courtyard. Hannah
passed them and went inside, leaving the car by the
shore. The locals turned to stare. Visitors usually fre-
quented the tourists' bars; this was scruffy and un-
spoiled. Hannah merely stared back and said with a
friendly nod, '*Buenas noches*.'

A plump landlady in a headscarf came to her table.
'You want to eat?'

Hannah replied in Spanish, 'Yes. What fresh fish have
you?'

'I have *mero*, but I paid *mil pesetas* for it.'

'That's OK.' Hannah ordered a bottle of Casal
Mendez, poured herself a glass of the sparkling pink
wine, and stared out of the window, down to the starlit
beach, the harbour with its forest of masts, and the dark

39

water beyond she could only hear, not see.

The woman lingered. 'You stay near here?' she
queried.

'I am not a tourist, *señora*,' Hannah told her. 'I am the
medico from San Agustín.'

'Ah, the *medico*.' That made her almost one of them.
The plump lady went off, satisfied, stopping to tell a
couple of the men who the visitor was. She brought
Hannah olives and new potatoes in their jackets, with a
chilli sauce to dip them in. 'Will not be long.'

She heard another voice speaking to the woman. He
said in Spanish, 'Give for me what you cook for the girl!'

Hannah knew his voice without turning round to look.
He ought not to have followed her. But her anger and
embarrassment had faded now, and her mind was
calmer and composed. She turned and gave him a cool
stare. He was wearing black jeans and a black short-
sleeved shirt. The gold chain hung outside the shirt, and
she saw there was a jewel hanging on it, that looked like
an amethyst. His hair was untidy, as usual, his eyes
masterful and direct. He stood taller than any other man
in the bar, both one of them, and yet their superior.

He did not take his eyes from Hannah as he pulled out
the simple wooden chair opposite to hers and sat down
without her permission. He gestured to the woman to
bring another glass, then said with triumph in his voice,
'So this is your friend, huh?' He still spoke in Spanish, as
he took her glass and drained it. It sounded more
commanding than his gentler accented English. 'You
drive out here and eat alone, and you tell me you have a
friend in Mogan. Why pretend, Hannah? Did you want
to get away from me?'

She returned his look, still inwardly calm. 'This is the
first time I've ever been here. Ask the woman.'

'So where does your friend live? On one of the boats?
And why did you not go to him tonight? Does he
entertain someone else on a Tuesday?'

Hannah retained her control. 'What does it matter to
you? You have your own amusements, surely, in San
Agustín. You should be far too busy with your own
"friend" to follow me all the way to Mogan just to see

who I meet. I'm not your nanny. It was you who said you
didn't want to come under my wing. So why don't you
just turn round and go back again, Riviero? I'm off duty.
I don't have to speak to you off duty.'

He smiled at her with proud eyes. 'I was right—you
certainly do not need any swordfish, my friend. What a
tongue you have!'

'Are you saying that to see if that was what upset me?'
asked Hannah coldly.

Ramón seemed surprised that she was facing him
calmly, without any sign of anger. He shrugged. 'Something made you run away. I was curious . . .'

She interrupted in fierce and fast Spanish. 'Riviero, I
am not used to being questioned and followed! I live
alone from choice, and I enjoy it. Just because you now
work with me it doesn't mean you live with me. That's
not part of the agreement. I eat where I like, go where I
like, and don't have to tell you about it first. Is that
clear?'

He smoothed his chin between his fingers, and there
was a softening of his eyes now, a gentleness under the
fierce brows. 'Your Spanish really is excellent. You
sound like a native of Canaria.' The woman brought a
second glass, and he poured out wine in both, then
raised his to her. 'I am sorry you cannot find your friend
tonight. But we will eat together as colleagues, no?'

Exasperated, Hannah said, 'You're asking my permission now, when you've already ordered? Riviero,
why are you so fickle? You're polite when I'm not
expecting it, and for the rest of the time you're as rude as
hell!'

He drank again before saying quietly, 'I thought I was
beginning to explain about that. I thought you were
beginning to understand. I wish I had died in India. I
wish they had left me to the vultures, instead of bringing
me back to a life I do not seek. I live not as I choose, but
as I must. Hannah, I am still dead. You must give me
time to learn to be human again.'

She recognised the pull of her emotions, her desire to
be gentle and nice with him. But she did not give in to it;
he would only hurt her again. 'You were very human

when Rosita was with you,' she remembered.

'Rosita Alfonso?' A slight smile came to his lips, stayed there for a moment, but he did not say more. He poured out the rest of the wine, and shouted in Spanish for more. The woman brought it at once. Then she laid two places, and brought in two plates of *mero*, fried whole and served with Canary tomatoes, peppers, garlic and a wedge of fresh lemon. 'So, we have *mero* and not swordfish—that is good. Come, my partner, eat. We will drink a toast to your friend.'

The fish tasted wonderful, but Hannah couldn't finish it. She picked at the bones, pushing them around the plate. She didn't notice him watching her, didn't see the sudden tenderness in those beautiful eyes. But she heard his voice, as though from a long way away. He was talking to her. 'Hannah, are you listening?'

She looked at him, not sure if he had spoken. He was frowning a little, as though what he had to say was important. 'Yes?'

His eyes seized hers, the way they had that first night, and he reached across to touch her hand with his. Hannah looked away. She was scared of gestures like that from this man—they only weakened her reso've, made her more easily hurt. She was just going to shake his hand from hers, as she would an unpleasant stinging insect, but there was an interruption, shouts from the group of men in the courtyard. 'There he is—Riviero from San Nicolás! It is the son. They said he had come back.'

'But he is dead. How can a ghost come back?'

Ramón stood up as some of the men entered the room. 'Chico, is that you?'

There was a chorus of replies. Hannah heard them saying, 'The son of the Brute is here . . . they say he is on our side . . . take care, he may be spying for the Brute.'

She heard Ramón speak. His voice was low, but he spoke with reason and authority and they were soon listening to him. 'I am not a spy, Chico. I have not been to San Nicolás, and I do not wish to go. But if there is a need, then I will go and speak for you. I do not stand for injustice, and never will.'

'Who is the *Inglesa*? We do not want her.'

'Leave her alone. She is my partner, and a good doctor. The way you are going, you will need all the *medicos* you can get. Do not be hot-headed, now. Do not spoil any plans by acting hastily,' cautioned Ramón.

'But you will help? You will not disappear?'

Hannah decided it was time she disappeared. It sounded as though the men were talking about Ramón's father, Benito Riviero. But they called him 'the Brute', and their voices were angry. Ramón had calmed them a little, but the mood was still ugly, and she was scared. She laid down two thousand-peseta bills and left the room. Nobody noticed her going, so busy were they gesticulating and shouting, with Ramón in the thick of it. He could handle them. She closed the door behind her.

Rosita was just coming out of the ward when Hannah arrived back at the hospital. 'The new patient is sleeping,' she told her.

'Thanks, Rosita. I'll take over. You can go.'

'I'll be back at seven to give her food.'

'How is she?' Hannah asked.

'The ankles are very swollen, the hands a little. Her heart rate is now normal, her blood pressure is stable at one-fifty over one hundred. Her anxiety is less since her husband came to see her.'

'It was smart of Dr Riviero to make the diagnosis,' Hannah remarked.

Rosita agreed. 'He is a very clever man, so kind.'

'You knew him before? He greeted you like an old friend.'

'Yes, I knew him. He was at school with my brothers. And my whole family work for his father in San Nicolás, except that the boys got the sack. The Brute sacks anyone who asks for more money.'

Hannah began to see how Ramón was being looked on as the only man who could control the brute of a father. 'Dr Riviero has not been to San Nicolás yet?' she asked.

Rosita shook her head, her face worried. 'He is such a dreadful man, Dr Hannah. When he finds out that Ramón is here, he will be very angry indeed. There will be much trouble, that I know.'

'Tell me about the father. He owns plantations, I know. Does he also own that factory? Does he work there?'

'He owns everything, but he never goes there. His managers work for him, and they are hated for it. He sits at home in the Villa Pandora and grows fat like a pig.' Rosita looked at Hannah again. 'I do not know how such a man can have a son like Ramón. Ramón is a saint.'

Hannah could not blame the girl for falling in love with Ramón Riviero. 'Well, maybe,' she said, and Rosita went off home. Some saint!—he had admitted himself that he was not yet human. Oh well, at least Rosita was there to care for his creature comforts . . .

Hannah spoke to the new patient next morning. 'I'm Dr Day. You feel better?'

'Yes, doctor. Can I go home, please?'

'Yes. But you must stay in bed.'

'Oh, but I cannot! My husband needs someone to cook for him.'

'He isn't a baby. He can do it himself.' Hannah knew it wasn't easy to get the men to work in the house, but she also knew it was vital. 'You'll be very ill if you don't rest until the baby is born.'

'But he . . .'

Hannah forgot her own troubles. 'Come now, you love each other, don't you?'

'Oh yes!'

'And you want a beautiful child?'

'Oh yes, doctor, we long for one.'

'Then you must tell your husband he must do what I say.'

'Yes, doctor. Thank you.'

Ramón did not mention the affair in the tavern at Mogan next time they met. The hospital was busier, and they had less time together. That meant there was no time to argue, and they got on well enough between the four of them, with Ramón fitting in with the routine, and having no time to talk of his own heartaches. Just once during the next week he said to Hannah, 'You are not curious about Chico and his friends?'

'I think I'm safer knowing nothing at all about your activities, Riviero.' Inside or outside the law, in or out of Rosita's bed—she wanted no part of it. And she was beginning to congratulate herself at having found the way to a decent sleep at night at last.

One evening Hannah had been off duty, and returned just as Ramón was putting his instruments away. 'I did not think there were so many people in San Agustín,' he sighed.

She smiled. 'I was only on the beach, Riviero. Why didn't you call me? You know I don't mind work.'

'You looked too peaceful. I did come down, but I had no heart to wake you.' He hung up his white coat, smiling at her discomfiture, to think he had seen her sunbathing in her own secluded spot, without the top of her bikini. Hannah met his glance. Perhaps it was her imagination, but his face was looking less haggard than when they had first met. The eyes were quicker to look gentle, and they had lost their black rings.

There was a sudden knock on the front door and Hannah went to unlock it. A man stood there in gaudy pink shirt and shorts, holding a hand to his jaw. 'You closed, love?' he asked, in a broad Liverpool accent. She looked pointedly at the door, and he nodded. 'OK, I'll come back termorrer.'

'It's all right. Have you got toothache?'

'No, love, it's me jaw—there's a big lump like.' And he removed his hand, to reveal a swelling just over the parotid gland. He winced as she touched it.

'You've got an infected gland here. I can start you on antibiotics. Just sit down for a moment.' She went in search of Ramón.

He agreed with the diagnosis. 'I can feel a cyst inside the gland. I think it had better come out—local anaesthetic.'

'Thank you, Riviero. I didn't like to suggest it, as you've had a busy day, but it's better to excise it than to put him on antibiotics.'

'If you didn't want to suggest operation, why did you call me?' There it was again, the ability to smile, to make a joke instead of a complaint.

'Get on with it, man, and stop scoring points!' laughed Hannah.

'Yes, chief.'

He removed the cyst deftly and quickly, and the patient was able to walk back to his hotel with only two small stitches to show where the swelling had been. Hannah said tentatively, 'I think you ought to be paid more when you operate.'

Ramón said gruffly, 'I'm not in the habit of working for money, Day.'

'I'll ask Pablo what the going rate is.'

'I'm not in need of money.'

'But you're a qualified surgeon. They should pay the correct fee.'

'Maybe a little one, but no overcharging, Day. The name of Riviero is rotten enough already in San Agustín. I have a big task on my hands to make it good again.' And she watched him go, conscious that he carried more in his heart than just the knowledge of his illness. His honour mattered too. He was reminded daily of the hatred the natives here felt for his father.

Hannah had made up her mind to ask Ramón no further questions about his father or his home. That was his own business. She spoke to him kindly and cheerfully about hospital affairs, but she clammed up when the conversation turned to Benito Riviero.

So it was with great apprehension that on the following sleepy afternoon Hannah took the telephone on her way to a lazy sit-down on the verandah. Carla had answered it, and she said, covering the mouthpiece, 'Oh, doctor, this man won't give his name. He wants to speak to the person in charge, and he sounds awfully angry.'

'Hello?' Hannah had a feeling that she knew who it would be.

'*Quien esta a cargo de este?*'

She spoke in prim correct English. 'I am in charge. I am Dr Day.'

'*Este* Benito Riviero. *Mi hijo, este alli?*' It was a loud and bullying voice, and Hannah resolved at once not to co-operate with it. She hated bullies.

'Dr Riviero is not here at present. Maybe you could try tomorrow.'

'Desde cuando esta alli?'

'I really don't know, Señor Riviero.'

She was keeping very cool in reply to his blustering Spanish. She was just going to put the receiver down when a hand came over it, and Ramón bent his head towards hers, whispering, 'I will speak. Thank you for trying to put him off.' His face was very close to hers. She felt the lock of hair fall against her face. It smelt of Ramón, and she longed to touch it . . . They seemed very close suddenly, both on the same side against a common enemy. His look to her was gentle, as he took the receiver from her, giving her fingers a slight squeeze as he did so.

'You know who it is, then?'

He smiled. 'I could hear his voice at the other end of the hospital!' Hannah turned to leave him in private, but he caught at her sleeve and hissed, 'Stay and listen. Then you will understand.' Obediently she stood. His private life was no concern of hers, but the stresses and strains he suffered were. As a colleague, she must know how far he could be put under stress without weakening.

He spoke. 'Padre?'

'Serpent of a relative, to be in San Agustín and not come to the Villa! What sort of son is this I have, to care nothing for his father? You know I need help in the business. I need you here with me. Now that you are sent home with illness, where else should you be but here with me? What will everyone think, that you came back to San Agustín, and do not make the journey to San Nicolás to your own flesh and blood . . .' He went on in this vein, with Ramón holding the telephone some inches from his ear. Hannah realised what a personality he was, why so many people loathed him, and why poor Ramón had an uphill struggle to give the name respectability.

This father and son were too far apart ever to be reconciled, yet Ramon was managing to get a word in. 'OK, OK, I had to get some work fixed up, but I'll be along. Yes, sure I mean it. No need to promise—when I give my word I mean it. Yes, of course medical work. I am not a plantation owner, Father. I'm trained to look after people, not tomatoes.'

The conversation went on in loud voices. Hannah decided she had heard enough, and left Ramón thumping the table with one hand to get his point across. She went out to the verandah, sat in her favourite chair, and tried to ignore the shouting from the hall.

Ramón came out at last, showing signs of being over-excited. 'You didn't stay with me.'

'There was no need, I could hear everything from here.'

He pursed his lips, smoothed back his hair. 'I do not want to go. You think I should go, Hannah?'

'You've given your word,' she shrugged.

'Will you come with me?'

'Me?' Hannah's voice rose to a squeak. 'Why me?'

'He might modify his language if I am with a lady.'

'I doubt it. He isn't a very polite man.'

Ramón laughed shortly. 'You noticed that. Well done!'

'I don't have any place in a family row,' Hannah said firmly.

He looked across at her under frowning black brows. His eyes pleaded for him and she knew she had no real choice. She knew she would go. 'You are my partner, Day. I owe it to you to show you why I have turned out so badly.'

'Oh, Ramón!' She wanted to run to him and hold him, but that was out of the question.

'That sounded very much like pity,' said Ramón ruefully.

She avoided his eyes, painfully aware of their message. 'No, it wasn't pity. But please don't hate yourself so much. It won't help.'

He sat down for a while, looking out to sea. The sky was cloudy, the sun yellow across the water. The beach was crowded. He said quietly, 'I feel like a whisky.'

'I know.'

He smiled mockingly. 'I thought you would say it was bad for me.'

'I'm not your nanny, or your conscience,' Hannah told him.

'You've said that before. Maybe I was hoping you would make a fuss, tell me I'm not allowed whisky? Maybe I was hoping someone would care.' His voice was hollow now, his eyes desperate.

Hannah stood up and went to the rail. Without turning she snapped, 'You know damn well we all care —Pablo and Dolores and me, Carla and Rosita—if your eyes were only open you'd see how we scurry around you as though you're important, damn you!'

'Skin-deep. You think you care, but it's only on the surface.'

Hannah knew what he meant. He yearned as she did for a deeper meaning to his relationships. Yet she knew she could not bridge the gap between them—not by trying to understand him now. What he needed now was encouragement to face what he had to face, both in life, and in San Nicolás. She said sarcastically, 'You don't make it any easier.'

Ramón stood up then, ran past her down the steps and towards the beach. She thought he had gone for a walk, but he was back in a few moments, carrying a bottle of Scotch by the neck. 'Join me, Day. What do you call it in English?—Dutch courage? Have some Dutch courage with me. Don't make me drink alone.'

They faced each other in silence, then Hannah turned and brought out two glasses, which she set on the table and sat down in the chair. She indicated the glasses with a flick of her wrist. 'I'll drink with you, glass for glass, Riviero. But for God's sake don't take the cork out with your teeth—that would be too much like the worst sort of Western!'

He smiled then, a genuine smile, showing his even teeth, crinkling his eyes, making him look younger, nicer . . . 'Querida, I have never in all my travels seen a whisky bottle with a cork. They all have to be opened like this.' And with a dramatic gesture he spun the top off and poured two inches of the spirit in each glass. 'Salud, querida.'

Hannah was still slightly punch-drunk from being

called darling. She picked up her glass, wrinkling her nose at the strong smell. '*Salud*. You do realise that it was only when you saw whisky that you smiled properly?'

Ramón looked down at her, the light still in his eyes. But then it died, as he raised his glass and said, 'To my beloved father.' He grimaced at the epithet and tossed off the neat spirit in one gulp.

Hannah had promised to match him glass for glass. She held it for a moment, murmured, 'To solving some problems, Riviero,' and put it to her lips. The smell made her eyes water. She sipped, unwilling to give in and spoil her dramatic gesture. She saw Ramón beginning to grin, and said stoutly, 'If you drink, I will.' And she tried to drink the whole lot without breathing, as one does with unpleasant medicine. The whisky burned her throat, but she finished it and set down the glass, blinking a little at the strength of it. She gasped, feeling the burning going on down her oesophagus, as though corroding the skin lining.

'More?' Ramón was standing by her.

'You want to drink until the pain goes away? It will still be there when you wake up with a headache.'

'More?'

'If you do.' The thought of imbibing more neat spirit appalled her, but she knew if she showed no interest, he would go on. 'Naturally.'

He had lifted the bottle, but her face made him pause. 'Oh, Hannah,' he whispered. It was only a whisper, but she felt a pulse of emotion in his voice. And he put the bottle down, together with his glass. 'Thank you for stopping me.' He walked to the front of the verandah and stood, both hands on the rail, his head bowed between his shoulders for a long time. His attitude made Hannah, after the drink, incredibly sad for him. She sat with tears in her eyes, unaware of the time. After a long time he turned and looked at her over his shoulder. 'You are still here?'

'Yes.'

'I'm sorry.'

'Don't be.'

He looked out again at the sea. 'I'm worth nothing, you know—nothing. Most people know that.'

'If you say so,' said Hannah quietly.

He turned round, leaning his back against the post with the bougainvillea. 'Come with me to the Villa?'

'I don't see how it would help.'

'Are you scared of him?' he asked.

'Does it matter?'

Ramón stood before her. 'I think so. You are sensible, Day, you don't allow anyone to get away with nonsense. I know that, to my cost. You—you——'

Hannah stared at him miserably. She could almost read his mind, feel his great need of her. His natural use of the word darling . . . '*Querida* . . .' had burst upon her consciousness. She had to go on doing her job, not relying on support from Ramón Riviera, because he might use the occasional word that sounded right—but most of the time he only needed moral support. Emotional support he did not need; he was immune. Life had made him like that—unable to depend on anyone . . . Yet he looked so very easy to like, easy to love . . .

A shout from down the path. '*Medico—Rapido! Medico!*'

She was alert at once. A man in waiter's dress was running along the path from the beach. 'Someone is ill—please come!' Hannah rushed for her bag, pulling on her white coat as she came down the steps. The man led the way to a café. 'A woman—they have taken her to the back . . .' She was lying on a rough coach. Suddenly she sat up, then screamed. Hannah reached her at once. There was little doubt of the diagnosis.

'She's in labour,' she said urgently.

'A baby? Here? Please not here, doctor!'

Hannah found she had to soothe the waiter as well as the woman, as the intense pain of a contraction passed off. 'Don't worry, we'll get her to the hospital. Ring the bell, *por favor*.'

Esteban heard the shouts, and was already on the way. He bent. 'Stretcher?' And within minutes he was back with it.

'Well done, Esteban!' she smiled.

'Thank you.' She looked up hastily from her patient. It was Ramón. 'We have an unexpected arrival, yes?' he queried.

'Yes, Ramón. Could you make sure we have a Simpson's forceps handy?'

Hannah and Esteban lifted the woman on to the stretcher. When the next contraction had passed, Hannah asked, 'What is you name? Where can I reach your husband?'

The woman screamed again as another contraction racked her body. It was more fear and shock that caused her shouts. Hannah soothed her as well she could. When she looked up again, Ramón was in his white jacket and sterile gloves. 'Let me see.' Hannah allowed him to take over. He had done this more often than she had, and in more primitive conditions. He examined very gently, and the woman sobbed quietly between pains, and seemed to relax a little, begin to trust him.

Within moments the patient was quiet. Hannah gazed at Ramón with sheer admiration. What a gift he had, by his very presence almost, of inspiring confidence and relaxation. The woman began to groan again, but without the panicky screams. Hannah was able to hold her hand and help her through the violent contraction while Ramón talked quietly, his words helping and encouraging her. 'Breathe through your mouth, my dear. Try not to push yet. Come, come, look out of the window, breathe, breathe and look at the waves on the shore. Gently, gently, my dear.' He checked the cervix again. 'Just another few moments, my dear. Come, they have sent for your husband. He will be here in time, don't worry.'

He murmured to Hannah so that the patient did not hear, 'The cord is round the neck. She mustn't push now—I'll try to move it. Talk to her, Hannah.' She saw perspiration on his forehead, as with infinite patience and dexterity he worked to free the yet unborn child. The minutes seemed to drag, the contractions came more frequently. But by the magic of his personality, the patient now was concentrating on doing what she was told, and between gasps, she managed to smile at

Hannah, who sat by her head and patted her hands.

The next contraction was a bad one. Hannah said, 'I'll give her some gas now?'

'Sure. Give her the mouthpiece, let her take it only when she needs it.'

'How's it going?' she asked.

'I think I've got it, if we don't get another contraction.' Ramón dashed the sweat from his face with his arm. Rosita quickly reached up and wiped his face tenderly with a tissue. The woman grunted suddenly, and Ramón said, 'Right, here we go. That's clever, my dear, very clever. Gently does it, very gently—and now push —push, push, push!' Guided by him, she seemed to know what to do instinctively now. With a great cry, not of pain but of effort, the little baby's head slithered out. Ramón's fingers were there, making sure the cord did not strangle it. And then came the tiny body, a perfect little boy. 'Wonderful, wonderful! You have a beautiful son.' He picked him up, gave the slimy little buttock a tap. Hannah was there with cotton wool to clean the mouth and nose. Ramón took a small blanket from her and wrapped the baby in it, as he coughed and gave a sudden loud wail.

The mother cried then, cried with tears of happiness and relief. Ramón placed the little bundle in her arms, and she bent and kissed the wrinkled little face. Ramón leaned over them both, smiling and gentle, while Hannah gazed more at him than at the child. What a difference in him now! Gone was the tough, alienated man she had first met, who could be cruel and hurtful and sardonic. His face now showed nothing but tenderness. He put his finger to the baby's cheek, and the minute hand gripped at it and tried to suck at it.

Ramón looked up suddenly and saw Hannah looking at him. He read her eyes, and she knew that he didn't want her to see that side of him, the human, tender side. He pulled off his mask and gloves and turned away, striding quickly from the theatre. Hannah let him go. She understood how he felt. She turned back to the human miracle he had just assisted in so wonderfully. She felt rather overwhelmed. She felt she had seen that day something very special and wonderful. Her throat constricted.

The mother was speaking now, her voice still sounding tired but very happy. 'He was not expected for another three weeks. I thought I had only the stomachache with eating lemons!'

Hannah brought herself back to reality. 'Shall I just check his little heart? And weigh him? You want to know how tough your son is, don't you?' She examined the baby, a perfect little specimen. 'For three weeks early he isn't even underweight. Well done, my dear. Now, I think I see a young man coming up the drive. Your husband is tall, with a moustache?'

'Oh yes.'

The father was surprised—and rather pleased that it was all over. As the mother put the child to her nipple, he asked, 'What name shall we give him?'

The mother had not doubts. 'Doctor, I would like to call him for the man who just went away. I want my son to be like him.'

Hannah's eyes filled, and her voice was a little strained as she said, 'His name is Ramón.'

Rosita came in with the one cot the hospital possessed, with hastily found sheets, and placed it beside the bed. 'You must want to sleep now, *señora*. I will bring you some tea, and small Ramón will sleep right beside you.'

Hannah left the new family in Rosita's care. She felt suddenly exhausted. It had been a tense few hours. She took a quick shower, then lay for a while on her bed. She did not go out as she usually did, because she thought Ramón might be there, and she respected his need for privacy just then. His armour had been breeched that afternoon, and she wanted to intrude on him no more that day.

The bell went at the front door and Hannah went to see two more patients. Then she locked up, hung up her white coat, and walked slowly back to the verandah, pausing only to look unseen at the patient. The husband was staring down at the sleeping baby, and she heard him say, 'I will stay until I see his eyes open again, Ana. I want him to look at me.'

Hannah walked down the beach path towards Pepe's. She looked back at the hospital, lit by the rays of the sinking sun. What a difference in the state of it, the state of her own mind, since the arrival of the tall stranger just a few weeks ago. He had shattered her peace. Yet he had also brought—what? She could only describe it as heart. Her hospital had a heart. Yet her own heart felt strangely twisted and wrung out—a high price to pay. Ramón Riviero had hijacked her peace.

She didn't stop at Pepe's, but went to the end of the beach path and out on to the grey sand dunes, that stretched for miles from San Agustín to Maspalomas. The low sun made rolling shadows on the dunes. The wide ocean was gentle tonight, the breakers quieter than usual. A single cactus thrust up its jointed arms into the sunset. Hannah walked, her sandals in her hand, her bare feet cool in the grey sand. She wasn't sure how far she walked, but when she turned to walk back, the lights of Pepe's bar couldn't be seen for rolling dunes.

She shook the sand from her feet as she climbed the steps to the verandah. She felt calmer now. She looked back at the dunes, looking like some great petrified ocean in the moonlight.

'Why did you walk so far?'

Hannah jumped. Ramón was sitting there in the twilight, and there was a glass of whisky at his elbow. 'I don't know,' she answered.

He was drunk, but in a sad, quiet way. 'Will you come with me to the Villa?' he asked.

'Now?'

'Not now. I have no courage yet.'

She felt closer to him, now that she had seen beneath his protective harshness. But she still felt unwilling voluntarily to get herself involved by making his father's acquaintance. Benito Riviero was someone she would like to avoid meeting for a very long time.

Just then two men came round the corner of the hospital, and Rosita Alfonso was with them. Ramón immediately ran down the steps, and the four heads were very close together. Hannah watched them for a

moment. It was clear that for the workmen of San
Agustín, Ramón was their great hope for reform in his
father's businesses. She looked at Rosita. She was lovely
in a white lace blouse and vibrant green skirt, her long
hair rippling down her back. Even as she watched,
Hannah saw Ramón put his arms, one round the man
next to him, and one round Rosita's shoulders as she
stood next to him.

She went inside then. She wanted nothing to do with
the conspiracy they seemed to be plotting. She sat at the
table in the kitchen and cut herself a slice of cheese,
nibbling at it without appetite. The whisky bottle was
three-quarters empty. Poor Ramón, having to fight
other people's battles as well as his own against his
illness!

Hannah heard his footsteps, light but firm. He called
her softly, and she said, 'In the kitchen.' He came in, his
hair untidy over his eyes, but his stance dignified, his
eyes proud. 'Have some cheese?' she offered.

'I am to eat with Señora Alfonso.'

'Then you'd better hurry up and mop up some of the
whisky.'

He sat down instead. 'Hannah, please say you will
come with me.' He was pleading now, openly begging.
'Just the once? The first time?'

She repeated what he had said earlier, 'Because you
think he might modify his behaviour if there's a lady
present?' She laughed. 'I see you only call me a lady
when you want something!'

Ramón stood up, his eyes fierce under the brows.
'You are a lady, Day. I have admiration for you. And I
admit my need of this one favour from you. I swear I will
not trouble you again.'

Rosita came in, hesitating when she saw Hannah.
'You are ready, Ramón?' He nodded, and turned to go
out with her. Hannah watched them go, knowing that
she would not deny Ramón what he wanted.

CHAPTER FOUR

THERE was nothing more said about visiting the Villa Pandora. But Hannah found herself thinking of it, knowing that one day she was going to have to meet that Benito—the Brute, who sounded like a cross between a steamroller and an angry bull. And she silently sympathised with Ramón, bearing the stigma of having a father who was hated by the whole community.

Meanwhile the hospital became busier, and its name began to spread, as Ramón's presence meant that operations could be done as well as minor complaints seen. He still refused to take more pay than she did. 'I enjoy it,' was all he would say.

There was a boy brought in after a motorcycle crash. His leg was badly gashed, and there were pieces of metal in the wound. Hannah tidied it up as much as she could, but he would have to go to Las Palmas for X-ray and more treatment. She was going to call Esteban back, but Ramón said, 'Let me see what I can do first.'

They took him to theatre, and Hannah watched Ramón closely. The wound was irregular, jagged and difficult to treat; operation would not be easy. But her colleague scrubbed up calmly, and proceeded to investigate every centimetre of the leg, probing carefully and removing minute scraps of metal with small tweezers. It took over two hours just to rid the wound of foreign particles. He then started to stitch the skin together, using small neat stitches, working in bouts, so that he could straighten his back every few minutes and look away from the delicate work.

When the last stitch was knotted, the leg looked something like a patchwork quilt. But there was no bleeding, and the leg once again looked like a leg and not a piece of meat. Hannah felt she ought to applaud. 'You are good, Riviero—really top class.'

'Not bad, was it?' He stood back as the boy was taken

back to the ward, and peeled off his gloves.

'A month ago you couldn't have stood an operation as long as that.'

He looked at his watch. 'You're right. I've got more stamina. I don't feel tired now.'

'You could move out and take a decent job now—no need to stay here if you don't want to,' she pointed out.

'Want to get rid of me, Day?' queried Ramón.

'Well—not really.'

'I should think not! Your hospital is getting famous because of me.'

'I know that, you modest shrinking violet. But you'd earn more like the salary you deserve.'

He stretched his arms and back. They walked out to the verandah without saying anything, reading one another's minds. 'I like it here,' he said. 'For one thing I'm slowly showing these people of San Agustín that Riviero isn't necessarily a dirty word. And for another thing—I can't move without Pablo's permission. I'm due for yet another of his interminable full blood counts.'

Hannah had almost forgotten that this man was still under sentence of death. 'Surely it must show some improvement? You're looking so much better.'

'We can only hope so,' Ramón replied shortly. It must be hard to hope, after all the months of illness and pain.

The sound of the guitar floated up to them from the beach café. Hannah found herself blushing, recalling the first time she had heard that old man playing. She still loved the music, but had steeled herself to expect no response from Ramón Riviero. He had taken her into his arms only that once, the very first time they met. And that was only a natural reaction, after his long abstention from women, she knew. 'That guitar is beautiful,' she said diffidently.

'Flamboyant. He is a little show-off, that Manuel. He knows that a single flamenco will win him the price of a bottle of cognac from those gullible tourists down there.'

Rosita came out to sit with them on the steps of the verandah. Even in a white overall she was gorgeous, a sight to please any man. After a while Hannah went inside to lie on her bed. She looked at herself in the long mirror—a slight pale creature compared with Rosita. And unsophisticated where love was concerned. Yet as the urgent notes of the guitar floated in through the open window, Hannah sighed, knowing she could soon become good at loving, if she were only given the chance . . .

The telephone rang and she jumped up to answer it, rather than disturb Ramón. It was Dolores. 'You have put me off long enough. I am cooking my best kebabs for you and Ramón next Wednesday. Surely you are getting on well now?'

'All right, I suppose,' Hannah told her.

'Good, then I will expect you both.'

Hannah went in search of Ramón, but Rosita said he had gone to shower. Hannah sat in her own chair and looked down at the pretty young face of the Canarian girl. 'Tell me about the Villa Pandora?' she invited.

Rosita shifted on the top step so that her back was against the post, her face towards Hannah. 'That place? It is the most hateful place on the island. Yet I suppose that inside, it is the most beautiful.' Her voice was sad. 'When the Brute made my father manager of one of the plantations, he spoiled his happiness. He always was asking for more profit, more profit. And when my father made the workers work harder, he refused to give them more money. He is like that, the Brute.'

'Poor Ramón, to have such a background,' commented Hannah.

Rosita agreed warmly. 'Poor Ramón. He is so kind, so good.'

Hannah looked down at the woman who was presumably giving Ramón sexual comfort. 'You like him very much, don't you?'

Rosita did not hesitate, 'Very, very much. The men too, they admire him now. They feel he will help them. At first they thought him too weak, but slowly he is meeting them, talking with them. They trust him now to save them.'

Hannah said wanly, 'He confides in you at lot.'

Rosita said quickly, 'If he does not confide in you, Dr

Hannah, it is not because he does not trust you, but because he wants to spare you from worry over him. He is a proud man. Ramón will never go looking for sympathy. He sees what has to be done—and he knows that only he can do it.'

'I can see that.' If she had hesitated before, Hannah knew she could not now. When Ramón went to the Villa Pandora, she would be at his side. She ought to be proud of being asked, instead of scared of meeting the Brute.

But when he asked, her heart still failed her. It took all her strength of will not to show her dislike of the trip. She had been on her way for her morning swim the following Wednesday, their day off. She was wearing her black swimsuit, and carrying her *pareo*. The morning was still misty, a little chilly yet, and the waves looked grey on the grey sand, rolling endlessly up the beach, falling back into the emerald ocean.

Ramón came out suddenly, calling her name, and Hannah turned. He was wearing only his black jeans. His chest was bare, and he was mopping his face with a towel after shaving. How could such a vital-looking being have a fatal disease? There was an aura of power around him, and she couldn't help staring at the perfection of his body. 'Come, the time is now. I have to do it. We will go to San Nicholás today.' The black eyes were blazing in the lean face, the nervous energy in him giving him the look she had seen in the eyes of a caged tiger.

'Ramón, it's six o'clock!' But her protest was muted by the fire in his eyes. And she knew she had to support him now—that he deserved support. In fact, she knew that Pablo would insist on him not going alone, on an errand where his physical and psychological strength were to be tested to the utmost. 'I'll get dressed.'

For the first time Ramón seemed to notice that she had very little on. His expression altered. His attention came back from the future, from his intended crusade —and focused entirely on Hannah Day. 'Beautiful,' he murmured. 'Day, do you know you are beautiful?'

She suddenly had him completely. She could see appreciation in his face, and it was a powerful feeling, a sudden delight. But other matters were pressing.

'Wednesday is my day for being beautiful.' She hoped it sounded off-hand—that his unexpected compliment meant very little to her . . .

He put out his hands and caught her naked waist with firm fingers. Then he laid his face down between her breasts for a brief moment, pulling her close. His face was warm and smooth and smelt of soap, and Hannah could have caught him, held him there, so sweet was the sensation. But then he let her go, slowly. Avoiding his look, she ran indoors, stumbling a little in her haste, back to her room. She stood for a while after closing the door, catching her breath in little sobbing gasps. He meant nothing by it—he just had a passionate nature, the continental facility for showing his admiration. But her ears throbbed with the blood from her excited heart, and the imprints of his fingers were still there, pink in the skin of her waist. She touched them gently, and felt her whole body yearn to have them there again.

She dressed carefully, in her simple blue cotton dress, with high neck and full skirt. She wore canvas shoes in blue, and tied her hair back with a narrow matching ribbon. She trembled a bit at the thought of going out there again. Her feet made no noise as she returned to the verandah, and saw Ramón standing at the rail, looking far out at the distant horizon. He had put his shirt on, thank goodness—a red silk shirt that made her think of a bullfighter. He sensed rather than heard her, and turned round on his heel. 'Come, we will start. Don't waste time eating—I will take you to a place in the mountains for breakfast.'

The doctor in her disapproved. 'And if you pass out on the way?'

'OK, OK, I know. Get us some juice, then. But hurry.'

'Typical—let the woman get the juice! You could easily have done it while I was getting ready.'

'Don't nag.' And she was already obeying him, with a smile on her lips. She didn't really mind getting him orange juice. She took two glasses out. He already had his car keys in his hand, and drank the orange in one swig. 'Ready now?'

Hannah put the empty glass on the table by his, and ran after him along the side of the hospital. It was still early. The cement lorries from Benito's factory had not yet disturbed the tranquil morning with their noise and their fumes and their dust. The sun was not yet up over the central hills, but the sky glowed now, heralding it, and the mists were dispersing, and Ramón's powerful little car sped round the bends along the Las Palmas road, turning off after a mile or so on to the Cerva de Spinas road into the mountains.

Drab grey rocks loomed on each side of the ribbon-like road, yet the dawn gave them a blue tinge of beauty. It was like a moon landscape. Hannah forgot that they were on a mission, and began to imagine them on a strange planet . . . The only green things along that dismal rocky road were giant cacti, clinging to the stony volcanic mountains like some extra-terrestial beings, waiting only for their bug-eyed general to land in a spaceship and give them the order to remove themselves from their perches and march against the human race. She looked sideways at Ramón, and decided that perhaps he would not appreciate her imagination at that moment, so she kept her fancies to herself as he drove on and on along the dry track.

The sun rose, flooding the grey scene with light. Ahead were a few small white square houses, set in the semi-desert. The rocks soared above them, making Hannah feel terribly insignificant in the universe. She looked again at Ramón, his profile set and determined, and felt safer. He turned and smiled. 'Not too far now. I want you to meet some old friends of mine.'

'I never imagined anyone living out here,' said Hannah.

'These are the true Canarians. They are not parasites living off bloated tourists, but real men and women who struggle for their existence against the desert.'

They swerved into the settlement, and Ramón slowed the car, came to a stop under a white pebble-dashed wall hung with glorious masses of scarlet geraniums and deep purple bougainvillea. He hooted the horn, and the echo of it went round the rocks. An old brown face peered down at them from over the wall. Ramón jumped out of the car and shouted up in Spanish, 'Ho, my uncle, you are pleased to see Ramón?'

The old man hurried down the steps at the side of the house, and was enfolded in Ramón's arms. Tears ran down his face. 'God bless you, God bless you, Ramón Riviero! We thought you had died in India.'

Ramón beckoned to Hannah. 'Uncle, this is my friend Hannah.' She liked that. Not partner, not even doctor —just Hannah. She smiled at the old man, and was rewarded by an approving grin.

The old man was wrinkled, but his face glowed with health. His trousers were held up with string as well as braces. His shirt was worn but clean, and his boots had seen better days. 'Come in, come in. Mia is waiting to see you.'

They climbed the concrete steps, between banks of geraniums. Aunt Mia stood in her full peasant skirt and apron, her arms outstretched to her dear Ramón. 'Come, you must have coffee, some food. You are very thin, Ramón. You too, Hannah, you are very thin.'

Ramón said, 'We will take some bread, *mi tia*, but we have a long way to go. We will visit Abuelo next, and then go down to San Nicolás. I have not yet visited my father.'

A look passed between the old people. Hannah spotted it, and said, 'Yes, we've heard from many people what he's doing. That's why Ramón has come.'

Ramón nodded. 'I want to be able to look my neighbours in the eye, Uncle. My father has to be told that I side with them, and that he cannot go on as he has been. He is still underpaying you, I can tell. What did he give you for the last lemons?'

'Riviero is no ordinary crook. He has bodyguards —dogs.'

Hannah saw Ramón wince. 'God, he must need them by now! But he bears my name, and I want it made clean.'

Aunt Mia took them to the front garden, where there was a wooden table under a lemon tree. There was a rusty tap in the corner, and some bright yellow and green finches were drinking from the tin bowl beneath it. She placed slices of watermelon, a plate of brown rolls, butter and honey on a white tablecloth. 'Aunt, this is a banquet!' Ramón called Hannah to eat with him, while Mia brewed some coffee.

'They are no relation of mine,' he told her. 'But in the old days, Marcos was close to my father. He and Rosita's father were school friends. Look at the shabby way he has treated them. They all worked together in the fields, but once the cement began making money for my father, he bought up the land, and employed his friends as labourers.'

Marcos brought out a tray with four mugs of coffee, strong and fragrant. 'What does your father do, Hannah?' he sat down with them.

'He is dead, *señor*. But he did what you did once —grew vegetables and fruit, and sold it at the market.'

The old man's face crinkled up in pleasure. 'So they do this in England too? Come and see my plot.' Hannah was flattered. She went with him to his field, where there were neat rows of maize, onions, carrots and asparagus. 'I used to have tomatoes, but now Benito has bought all the plantations, and he sells them below my price. It is no longer worth the trouble. Lemons, too, he has almost a monopoly, and bananas. This tiny plantation gives us only enough for ourselves and our neighbours.'

As they left the little house, sweet-smelling and cheerful with the song of the finches, Marcos pressed an armful of lemons into Hannah's hands. 'There, you will not get them so good in the market.' And as they waved goodbye, Mia called, 'Give our love to Abuelo.'

They drove some way into the hills without speaking. Ramón said, 'You don't have to clutch those lemons all the way there.'

Hannah laid them on the shelf. 'They feel warm and natural, and they smell nice.'

He looked at her, his eyes lingering for a moment. There was a feeling of closeness with him. She was glad she had come. She was proud he had brought her to meet the people who mattered to him. But she did not try to put it in words. Even now she knew that Ramón Riviero had the power to hurt her feelings if she showed them too clearly. So she turned her gaze back to the road ahead, narrow and unmade, and beginning to rise up into the hills. It was very narrow, and the bends were sharper. Hannah was on the outside, and the precipice was just beneath her. She closed her eyes.

'You are afraid?'

Hannah opened her eyes. 'I'm terrified of heights.' Ahead the mountain rose higher and higher, and the road clung to its side looking only the size of a goat track. 'Are we really going up there?'

'Hold on—I know the road. You will be safe.'

'Unless I die of fright!' Her voice was tense in her throat as she tried to make light of it.

On and on they climbed, mainly in first gear, the engine whining as they rounded corner after corner, rising to the blue mountain peaks themselves. And still they climbed, each range giving way to yet another, until the drone of the engine had drilled into her very soul.

They came to a place where the road widened, and Ramón drew in to the side, parked by a prickly cactus. 'We'll wait here for a while. You will be stiff from sitting all screwed up in your seat.' His face was sympathetic. He went round and opened the door for her, and she climbed out, her knees trembling. He put his arm round her and led her to a convenient rock, where she sank down gratefully, glad of the pause in the drone of the engine.

Ramón said, 'I am feeling very weary. Will you take over?'

Hannah tried not to gasp with disbelief. Drive? Up there? yet another peak loomed before them, and she could see where the road wound round in hairpin bends. But if he needed her—it was better to go on rather than back. She tried to keep her voice steady. Ramón was a sick man. It was safer for her to take over than run the risk of him collapsing over the wheel. 'Yes, all right. Give me a few minutes.'

And then she looked up, to see him grinning broadly, leaning casually on the car. 'You are quite a girl, you know. Scared to death, yet you would have taken over, wouldn't you?'

Hannah forgot her fear in her relief. 'That was a dirty trick, Riviero! If I wasn't so scared of going near the edge, I'd hit you for that!'

'You ought to have known I wouldn't trust my precious car to a mere woman,' he grinned.

'You beast! Not only could I take over now, but I could probably drive better than you.' He nodded, as though pleased, and she realised why. 'I see—by making me annoyed, you've taken away my fear. Well done! A psychologist as well as a surgeon.'

'You are ready to go on?'

She stood up, took two or three deep breaths. The air was fragrant and fresh. Above them the crags were blue and beautiful. And from one rock towered a slim silvery cross, casting a delicate shadow on the mountainside. 'I'm ready.' As they both got in, Ramón reached over and fastened her safety belt for her. She shivered at the touch of his hands across her body, then said, 'You really are a bit of a fiend, you know. I never know when you're joking and when you're deadly serious.'

'I know, but I can't change now. It's too late in my life. I'll have to remain a fiend.' He started the engine and looked across—and said softly, comfortingly, 'Not much farther now.'

'I don't believe you any more. We'll go on driving in these hills until the sun sets and until we drop off the edge of the world.'

He looked at her for a second. 'It sounds quite a nice way to go.'

'Don't you dare talk like that again!' It hurt her to talk of his death.

'Sorry.'

They went on. He was right: soon they began to descend slowly, and turned away from the precipice into a path lined with bamboo and cacti on both sides. Ramón said quietly, 'You were very scared.'

'Yes. Do we have to go back the same way?'

'No, we go back by way of San Nicolás. The mountains are less steep there, and the road is smooth. But we meet my father—that might make you wish we had come back this way. The danger is less than meeting him.'

'You make it sound like *The Pilgrim's Progress*! You know, with giants and quicksands round every corner.'

'In a way it is. I am the pilgrim, and this is the road I have to take.' Ramón looked at her briefly. 'I realise I made it very difficult for you to refuse to come. I really gave you no choice.'

'Yes, Riviero, I did notice that. But you're so used to getting your own way that I didn't even care.'

'Oh, you can rail at me again now—now that you are no longer afraid of the mountains! Go on then, nag away—your favourite pastime.'

'You like it, don't you? It will help you to face your Giant Despair, just as your joking with me helped me to forget my terror.'

'Yes.' His voice held a note of tenderness then. 'I was cursing my fate, you know, that day I walked down the path to the hospital at San Agustín, and saw a girl there with a basket of strawberries.' He paused, negotiated another sharp bend on the way down. 'Do you think we are any better friends today than we were then?'

Hannah didn't answer, suddenly choked. Friends they might not be. But she knew her feelings were too deep to describe. This tall lean panther of a man with his good looks and tragic black eyes, who had walked down that path and into her heart and soul—there would be no escape from him, nowhere on the earth where she would be able to forget him now. He was part of her very being.

'My grandfather lives here.'

She had thought them in the middle of nowhere, but now she saw that the sides of the mountains were cultivated, blossoming with fruit trees, maize, tomatoes and strawberries. The bamboo was taller and thicker here. And beyond it were a dozen palm trees with green papayas clustering round the top of the trunk under the floppy leaves. In a moment they were in the middle of a small village, with chickens rooting in the middle of the dusty road, and several small white houses, shuttered against the sun.

Ramón jumped out of the car, and Hannah followed him, surprised by three white goats that suddenly came out of the bamboo beside her, followed by a shrivelled old lady in a black headscarf. Ramón said, 'Milking time, Abuela?'

The old lady screwed up her eyes and said in a cracked voice, 'You know me?'

'You have forgotten Ramón Riviero?'

'Ramón?' She peered at him again with short-sighted eyes. 'Dear Mother of God, it is Ramón!' She clung to him for a moment. 'Wait, I will tell Francisco. He sleeps always under the lemon trees in the afternoon.'

But Ramón's grandfather had heard the arrival of strangers, and he came out of the grove, shading his eyes from the sun. 'Ramón, I am blessed indeed to see you again before I die.' Ramón hugged the old man wordlessly, and Hannah saw tears roll down his dark cheek. 'Come and sit with me, Nieto. How many worlds have you seen, when I have not yet seen Las Palmas?'

'How are you, Abuelo? You still walk without a stick? Well done, old man.'

'Ninety-two, Ramón.' He was smiling, showing very few remaining teeth, when he saw Hannah, who stood back a little. 'What, Ramón? You have a wife to show me?'

Ramón took Hannah's hand and led her forward. 'A friend. Hannah is a doctor at the hospital where I work in San Agustín.'

Francisco held out both his hands to take hers within them, and shook them warmly. 'Since when do they use schoolgirls as doctors?'

'I'm nearly thirty, *señor*,' Hannah told him.

'And I am Abuelo, not *señor*.'

She smiled. He was lovely. 'I'm so very glad to meet you.'

The old man sat down on the soft grass beneath the trees, and his visitors sat with him. 'You must have food, and cold wine.'

'We cannot stay long,' Ramón told him. 'We are on the way to the Villa Pandora.'

The old lady was already bringing out an earthenware

jug of wine and four glasses. Francisco said, 'Cheese, Emilia, and some bread and onions. Hannah, try this wine—it is my favourite Rioja. I never thought I would live to drink it with my dear grandson again.' He shot a sharp glance at Hannah. 'You see, I have a grandson, but I have no son. There is only a savage who lives down the mountain, but he is no blood of mine.'

Ramón said warmly, 'Abuelo, some people are born without eyes, some people are born without hearing. Your son was born without a heart—but it is no fault of yours.'

'If you can change that heart of his, I will die happy. I think you are the only one who can.'

Ramón had eaten a small piece of bread and cheese. Now he drained his glass. 'We must be on our way. Hannah is too scared to ever come up in the hills again, but I will come again.'

The old man turned to Hannah. 'What do you say, *señorita*? Will you visit me again?'

'I would love to,' she smiled. 'I will not be afraid the second time.'

He held out his hands, one to each of them. 'I will not stand up—my legs know that this is their place in the afternoon. God go with you.'

They went back to the car without speaking. Hannah sensed that his heart was as full as hers. In this one day he had told her the story of his life, while saying nothing. It was all too clear, the tragedy of the one man who had poisoned this Eden.

Before they got back in the car, Ramón pointed out the small white church, the school, with goats grazing in its grounds. And even while they looked, a convoy of jeeps wound its way up the path from San Nicolás, each one full of tourists. They stood back, while the jeeps halted for the occupants to get out and take photographs. They giggled and talked. Several of the men carried beer in cans, and two of the women were smoking. They waved cheerfully at the couple, and Hannah waved back, but Ramón acted as though they were not there.

She knew how he felt. They were like clouds passing over the face of the moon. Ramón saw only the great moon of his crusade; he had no time for trivialities. As soon as the convoy had passed, he started the engine and they began the descent to the valley of San Nicolás. They passed a reservoir. There were four more jeeps there, and groups of people picnicking. He ignored them, pressing the accelerator as hard as he could between bends. His father's house was closing in on them, and he sped to his destiny like some landlocked Flying Dutchman.

As they descended, the grass and bamboo faded, leaving only the bare rocks and scree, the greyness only livened here and there by cacti. They came to a place where the road forked, and Ramón drew the Alfa to the side of the road and parked. 'Do you want to stretch your legs again?' he asked.

There was a heaviness in his manner, in his eyes. Hannah looked pitifully at him, wishing she could hold him, comfort him. 'I thought you wanted to get there.'

He leaned on the roof of the car. 'I wish I was going the other way.' He walked across to a low wall, where he leaned his elbows on it and stared down into the valley, where a small town lay as though made of toy houses. Hannah went over to stand beside him, and for a while neither spoke. She felt very close, as though every thought she could read, as his sad eyes roved over the distant valley.

She said suddenly, 'Ramón, you should have asked Pablo to come with you. He has been your friend much longer than I.'

Ramón picked up a piece of dry bamboo and began stripping the dried outer sheath from each segment, revealing the clear shining wood beneath. 'I find it hard to be comfortable with Pablo.'

'But why?'

He faced her, his eyes keen under the straight brows, intense and burning in the thin face. 'He does not know—that I know—that I will die.'

Hannah looked away, unable to face the emotion in his eyes. Ramón said, 'But he has told you, hasn't he? I see it in your face.'

'Dolores told me,' she admitted.

'You see how those two already carry my troubles for me? Pablo would have come, had I asked him. He would come to the end of the world for me. That is why I did not ask him.' Then he said gently, 'I did want you to come—to see . . .'

'Thank you,' she said softly. 'I'm glad.'

'You have met my abuelo. I wanted that.' Ramón straightened his back and said, pointing to a road sign, 'There is time to change your mind, and I will not blame you. That way lies Mogan, that way San Nicolás. I want you to decide. Shall I take the Mogan road?'

Hannah gave a little smile. Then she looked up at him and said firmly, 'Fasten your shoelace before you trip over, man, and let's get going before it gets dark. I'm hungry!'

Ramón bent and retied his shoelace, catching her up just before she got to the car. He caught her by the waist, pulled her towards him and turned her into the circle of his arms, kissing her mouth suddenly, wildly, hungrily. She put her arms round him, held him close as she had wanted to all day, touching his wild hair, stroking it, responding to his kisses without restraint. She felt protective, yet protected. Her head reeled with the sweetness they shared, locked together briefly on that silent mountainside, with the little town beneath them basking innocently in the sun.

CHAPTER FIVE

THEY followed the road to San Nicolás, saying nothing. It wound slowly downwards, with no frightening precipices, only rough rocks and stones. Then Hannah noticed that the whole valley was turning green. Water flowed in pipes alongside the road. Fenced and walled plantations appeared, with neat rows of well-watered trees and plants. There was real grass at the roadside, tall palm trees and graceful casuarinas and banyan trees. San Nicolás was a fertile valley, blessed with a decent water supply. Bright birds flew in the trees.

Hannah felt for Ramón, as he drove steadily round the bends, knowing and recognising the twists and turns of his childhood. He must be able to see the Villa now, recognise where his father lived among the jumble of orange-tiled roofs. But he kept his eyes on the road, his lips pressed tightly together, his eyes hooded, his face grim.

They passed poor houses first, small square rooms built into the side of the mountain, then richer homes, with walled gardens, luxuriant with ivy, with bougainvillea and with decorated wrought-iron gates. A white horse trotted proudly in the green fields, ridden by an equally proud-looking woman in immaculate breeches, her glossy hair piled up over a made-up face. She rode off into a plantation of banana and papaya trees. So Benito was not the only wealthy landowner here.

The walls got suddenly higher, with iron spikes along the top, and Hannah knew, without a word being spoken, that they had reached the Villa Pandora. Inside the wall she could see the tops of decorative cedars, palms and laurels. But when they came suddenly to the gate, there was no wrought iron, no ornament—only sheet metal, topped with barbed wire, with three padlocks, and at the side an intercom system, for them to announce their arrival. Ramón drew up with a screech of brakes and a flurry of dust. She saw he was gripping the wheel so that his knuckles were white. He said in Spanish, 'There she is. What a sweet family home!'

He got out of the car. But before he could move, a guard appeared through a small door in the wall—a guard in khaki uniform, with a shotgun in his hands and two black Alsatians snapping by his side, Ramón turned to Hannah, his face haggard. 'Welcome to . . .' And, suddenly overcome, he turned away, leaned his arm against the wall and his head on his arm.

Hannah stood in the dust, the late afternoon sun warm on her head and arms. Her heart went out to him, to the nature of his homecoming, the inevitability of this moment. They had both known it would be hard, but she looked up again at the sheet metal of his front entrance and felt sick with disgust. Ramón was not moving, just standing still, his head on his arm in an attitude of total dejection and surrender. She turned and said to the guard, 'This is Dr Riviero.'

The man looked from Ramón to her, back to the still figure. 'Dr Riviero?' He didn't seem sure what to do.

Hannah said, 'Telephone.'

Ramón turned slowly, dashing the tears from his cheeks. 'Telephone! Ask my father if he will let me in.' The moment of weakness had passed and he was in control of himself.

The gate swung open electronically. The two dogs were still wary, standing with ears cocked, their great mouths open in the heat, showing white teeth and hanging tongues. Ramón straightened his back and strode ahead through the gate into a drive and a garden of unspeakable beauty and elegance. Hannah walked behind him, nervous but not afraid. The guard could be heard putting chains into place behind them.

There was a central lawn with a fountain. There were shady nooks everywhere, with marble statues of gods and cherubs. Exotic birds fluttered and posed, with peacocks and pheasants stalking haughtily over the lawns. Around the lawn were tapering conifers. The path led straight now, past terraces of orchids and geraniums in all colours from white to deep red. The double front doors were louvred—wide open. Ramón strode on, oblivious of the beauty, while Hannah followed, her own head erect, showing no deference to the opulence around her. It was only money—and she knew that it was money that ought to have been shared more fairly.

Ramón made a striking figure as they went in from the brilliance of the sunlight into the shaded hallway. The crimson of his shirt was almost luminous, and the fire in his eyes cowed even Hannah at that moment. She stood back. Suddenly she felt she ought not to witness the meeting of father and son.

Ramón had not hesitated in the grand hall, but made straight for a panelled wooden door marked simply '*Privado*'. He pushed at it. A very fat man was just opening it, and the two stood face to face. Benito was tall as well as fat, and his bulk dwarfed the slim figure of his only son. There was anger and fire in his piggy eyes too. For a second or two neither moved, then Benito opened his arms and embraced Ramón.

Hannah knew she ought not to be there. She slipped out again into the garden. The dogs had disappeared, thank goodness. She made for a leafy bower, where a couple of vivid toucans sat on a wall and preened themselves with their huge painted beaks. She saw a gardener pass by with a wheelbarrow and eye her curiously, but she took no notice. She would be able to see when Ramón came out. It would soon be over.

Just then there was a little cough and she turned to see an elderly butler in neat white jacket standing respectfully close by. 'You are Dr Day?'

'Yes. How do you know?'

'From my niece, Rosita Alfonso. She told me you would be coming.' He said confidentially, 'We have been waiting for this day—for Ramón. Now we are confident that things will get better.'

Hannah said diffidently, 'I have nothing to do with your private problems. I know very little about them.'

'Rosita said you are a fair-minded lady. She said you were on our side.'

'I really . . .'

'You will take a message to Ramón for us?'

She looked at his sweet face, the silver hair lit by the sun looking like a halo. Behind him, she saw that the gardener had come to listen, standing meekly, his cap in his hands. The feudal system was still alive and well. She had to help to give these men their rights. 'I'll take a message, yes,' she agreed.

The old man looked nervously at the house, then handed her a paper. 'We do no wrong, *señorita*. All we ask for is modern wages. Our master only says, if you do not like it, go and work for someone else, but he knows there is no one else.'

'What is this paper?' asked Hannah.

He lowered his voice to a whisper. 'It is all the names of those who are with us—all who are willing to join in a strike.' He pointed to the first names. 'The first is Rosita's father, my brother. Even he has now been removed, for daring to stand up for his men.'

'Surely the government . . .'

'The Brute does not respect the government. Only money.'

Suddenly the men melted away into the shadows. Hannah heard footsteps on the path. A bright parrot fluttered and squawked, disturbing the toucans. And there was Ramón, side by side with the fat man. 'Hannah, come and meet my father,' he said.

She couldn't tell from his voice how the meeting had gone. She stood up and shook hands with Señor Riviero. He bowed before shaking her hand. 'I am honoured, *señorita*.'

'How do you do?' She kept her voice neutral, taking her cue from Ramón.

'Now, you must stay to dinner.'

That was an easy one. 'I'm sorry, but we're on the way to Dr Rodriguez for dinner.'

'Then please—come in for a moment and chat. I have the best sherry in the country, and some excellent caviare.'

She looked at Ramón, who gave an imperceptible nod. 'Thank you.' She walked by the fat man's side back to the house. 'You have a magnificent home.'

They walked in, making polite and meaningless conversation. It was a civilised and tolerant meeting; Hannah could scarcely imagine that this was the man whose voice had shrilled with passion and rage over the telephone.

They sat in a gracious drawing room, decorated like a Georgian salon, the delicate mouldings on the walls and ceiling picked out in white and gold. Soft music came from a hidden speaker. The deferential butler came in with a silver tray containing several carafes of sherry and crystal glasses. He gave Hannah a special smile as he served her, while Benito ignored him. 'You have been long in San Agustín?'

'Five years.'

'Without a partner?'

Hannah smiled. 'Mine is only a small clinic. I only bought it as a way to stay in the sun and do as little work as possible. I'm not ambitious, Señor Riviero. I believe in taking life as it comes.'

The fat man laughed. 'You do not have to explain that attitude to me. All Spanish people believe in *mañana*, you know. It comes naturally to them.'

'But the great explorers and conquistadores came from Spain.'

He liked that. 'They did. Maybe I have some of their blood.'

Ramón tried to stem the self-glorification. 'Our people are peasants, Father.'

'Nonsense, son.' Benito was smiling, but the steel behind his façade was immediately evident. 'There are peasants—and there are masters. It is in the genes. You cannot go against the genes.'

Ramón drained his glass. 'We must talk again, Father.' He stood up. 'Since I came back, I have heard stories about you. You have sacked many people.'

Hannah detected an atmosphere. Both men had forgotten she was there; suddenly they were confronting one another, both determined, both sure they were right. 'Ramón, I have only pruned down my work-force —I have to make a reasonable profit.'

'Why?'

'You are my heir. What else do I leave you?'

'I want nothing from you except a name—I want to inherit a name that is respected, not feared and hated. Do you know, Father, when I went into the tavern in Mogan I was almost set upon. That is what the name Riviero means in Mogan!'

'There is no unrest, son,' soothed Benito, 'only a handful of Communists who try to make trouble. You will soon get used to San Agustín again. Why will you not come and live here in comfort and style?'

Ramón turned away. 'I am a surgeon. What does a surgeon do on a plantation?'

Benito's voice was hard. 'There is a great amount of responsibility here—lands, monies, trusts and companies. One day you will have to administer it. You should already be studying how to do it well.'

'I'll manage.'

'How can you speak with scorn against your father? Your father, whose every move was made for you and for your future.'

'For your own glory, I think,' shrugged Ramón.

'What a repayment for all my hard work!' Benito exclaimed angrily.

'You paid for my education, that is all.'

Hannah rose quietly and went to the front door. Neither of them needed her; the conversation was getting heated, and she had no place in it. The butler came up to her. 'Señorita Day, we are so very hopeful now,' he told her.

She nodded. Ramón had put his case, but it was plain that Benito was certain he was right. Neither would give in. The errand was fruitless. But she didn't have the heart to say so to this old man with hope in his eyes.

Ramón came out like a crimson whirlwind, flinging the double doors wide. 'Come—we are going,' he said tersely.

She ran after him, her legs unable to keep up with his long strides without running. The gates were closed and locked. But the guard saw them coming, saw mastery in Ramón's face and ran to open them, to give a respectful salute before closing them again. They were in the car and driving off before Ramón said almost to himself, 'He will not change. He has an empty space in his brain where the common sense should be. Talking will never move him.'

'I know,' agreed Hannah.

'What can I do? Mobilise the workforce in defiance, and risk them all losing their jobs and livelihood?'

'You know you can't.'

'I know, I know.' And he said no more as they drove down to Mogan, and along the coast road to San Agustín. The sun set in one of its best exhibitions of colour Hannah had ever seen, yet even its magnificence could not lift their depression. Hannah knew quite well she had been dragged into politics without wishing to be. She fingered the paper in her pocket. Now was not a good time to give it. In her professional judgment, Ramón had taken enough today. He needed to wind down, to rest and take time to decide what next to do.

They came to a stop in the scrub beside the hospital. Home . . . She looked up at him, and cursed herself for not driving. He looked exhausted. She ought to have realised how much that exchange had taken out of him. She said, as they both sat without getting out of the car, 'I'll phone Dolores. She'll understand that we're too tired to go round.'

Ramón straightened his shoulders. 'No, I want to see them. I want to talk with sane people, after the day I have had.'

Hannah noticed that he didn't ask her what she wanted to do, but she forgave him. The situation was more than she could have coped with in his position. Poor gentle Ramón! All he wanted to do was be a doctor—something he did so well, something that brought out the full capability of his sensitive nature. She had seen it so often in the weeks they had spent together. She said quietly, 'I'll be out of the shower in ten minutes.'

She sat on the verandah in the starlight, waiting for Ramón to get ready. She was wearing her best green silk, feeling fresh and revitalised after washing the dust of the mountains from her hair and eyes. She put up her hair in a loose bun, and wore her only good earrings, heirlooms from a distant great-aunt, pretty hoops of emeralds and diamonds.

When Ramón came out there was nothing left of the flamboyant crimson and black. He wore a sedate cream shirt and black tie, with light brown trousers. He stood for a while looking down at her. 'Well, we didn't quarrel, did we? Being together all day?'

Hannah said stiffly, aware of the depth of emotions they had passed through together, 'Not even I could nag you on such an errand.'

'Thanks for that.'

It was as though they could not discuss it now, as if suddenly they were emotionally exhausted. She stood up and took the key from his hand. 'I'll drive.' He made no protest, and she watched him uneasily. He walked erect, but his step was slow. She must make sure they did not stay late at Pablo's house.

Dolores understood what they had been through, and didn't press them to speak about Benito. She understood, from the few comments Ramón made, that the mission had been unsuccessful. She spoke of smaller matters, treating them both rather like her own children, to be embraced and cared for and understood. After the meal they sat in the garden, the men wandering down to the small orchard at the end. Dolores said to Hannah, 'So you did speak to Benito?'

'I personally? Only small talk. He was polite, but I could see he didn't give a damn about anyone else but himself.'

Dolores looked at her keenly. 'You have been very good to Ramón.'

Hannah smiled ironically. 'I know that.'

'He does appreciate it, I know.'

'He accepts it. I'm just like some handy aunt.'

'He had nowhere else to go, you know,' said Dolores. 'You won't get too fond of him, will you? You are spending more time together.'

'I have no intention of getting fond of him,' Hannah assured her.

'That's good—I mean, for your own peace of mind.

Spanish men can use women—without meaning to, I mean, especially foreign women. They can protest all sorts of undying affection—I've seen it—but they do not marry them. They always turn back to their own race for wives.'

Hannah was sardonic. 'Marry? That one? Dolores, you must be joking!'

'No, not entirely. I could see, somehow—maybe it was the way you looked at him—the way you drove him here, walked beside him in case he needed you to lean on. I pray you are not in love without knowing it. I do not want you to be hurt.'

'I'm only taking a friendly interest, after all he has been through today.'

'Good. I think he looks better, Hannah. I think his next blood test will show some improvement, you know. But he resists having the tests, because he is afraid of it showing more damage.'

Hannah said diffidently, 'Dolores, does Pablo say he could get better—really better? Or is there no hope in the long run?'

The older woman looked at her with sympathy and understanding. 'It really is getting to you, Hannah dear. I didn't think—I mean, Pablo said you were too sensible to get involved.'

'Involved—come off it, Dolores, there's a man dying here . . .' Hannah had raised her voice, and she stopped, embarrassed. 'Sorry, it's been a tough day.'

Dolores said quietly, 'Pablo says he still could recover. He has youth on his side, a good constitution —does not drink or smoke. He has made already more progress than we had hoped. Yes, Hannah, he might make it.'

'Good. Then as soon as his blood test shows some improvement get him out from under my feet!' Hannah spoke vehemently. Dolores' dark eyes were troubled as she looked down the garden at the two men, walking together among the palm trees.

'I'll go and get some coffee.'

Pablo looked round, as though at an agreed signal. 'I'll give you a hand,' he said. They went indoors together. Ramón was standing under a palm tree, his hands in his pockets. He looked across at Hannah and her heart turned over as he smiled at her. 'Tired, Day?'

'It's been some journey. Your uncle Marcos, your sweet grandfather . . . I think I'm still in some sort of trance . . .'

'Yes—I'm tired, but my brain is still buzzing. We've still got a long way to go.'

'Correction—you have. It's not my war,' said Hannah.

He looked across at her again, the moonlight catching his face, highlighting the cheekbones, the lean jaw. 'We're friends, aren't we?'

'Maybe.' She thought back to the passionate embrace they had shared. She cared for him, yes. But friends? Surely a friend was someone she could confide in, tell her troubles to? And she would think twice about doing that to Ramón Riviero.

He was distracted from answering, as Pablo came out—not with coffee, but with a syringe in one hand, a gauze pad and a small bottle in the other. 'Oh no—not another FBC, Pablo! It's too soon. It will show nothing new.'

'Don't argue, man. I need it for my records.' Pablo winked at Hannah. 'Have you seen yourself in the mirror lately? You look a hundred per cent better. There's bound to be a change.'

'Leave it for another week,' urged Ramón.

Pablo joked with him. 'Ramón, you are a grown man. Look at this coward, Hannah, scared of the needle!'

Scared of death, more likely. Hannah moved instinctively nearer to Ramón. He bared his arm with a gesture of defiance that ripped the shirt sleeve as he pulled it back. 'Here—chronicle my deterioration if you wish. But don't tell me what you find!'

'I promise.'

Ramón stood holding his own arm still while Pablo found the vein, swabbed, and drew off a syringe of dark blood. He carefully released the liquid into two bottles. 'Keep them moving, Dolores, until they can be tested,' he ordered.

'The technician is calling in a few minutes.'

Ramón laughed without mirth. 'You have got this well planned, my friend.'

'It seemed like a good idea, as you were coming to see me tonight.' Pablo was irrepressibly good-natured, the perfect friend for Ramón, and he took his arm while Dolores brought out strong coffee, and more gentle chat.

They didn't stay long after that. Hannah could see that Ramón was weary, drained of energy. She went first to the car, not belittling him by holding him up. But she was touched when he did not hide his weariness from her in the car. He said sleepily, 'I couldn't drive now if you gave me a million pesetas.'

Hannah wound down the window, thanking the couple, and whispering to Dolores, 'I want to know the results.'

Her friend nodded. 'I'll ring you.'

Back at the clinic, she did give Ramón her arm, putting it round her waist as she had that first day when he collapsed at her feet. She took him through into the room he used when not at Señora Alfonso's, and he almost fell on to the bed. He put up a hand to pull off his tie, but was asleep before he could remove it. Hannah stood for a moment, watching him. He looked uncomfortable. She unbuttoned his shirt and slipped it off, then she unzipped his trousers, pulling them carefully off and putting them over the back of a chair with his socks. He lay in his black pants, legs straddled on the bed, handsome face unworried in sleep. His body was lean but healthy, his muscles rounded, his legs long and strong. She stood for a while, just looking at his face. So vulnerable now; so courageous and well-meaning he had been that day.

She drew a thin coverlet over him, feeling the overwhelming emotion that he was living with—the delicate tightrope between life and death. No one yet knew which way he would fall. She touched his face, suddenly very precious in his gentle sleep, and whispered 'God bless you,' in English. This vital life was too valuable to lose. Please let it run its natural span . . .

'Hannah?'

She had moved to the door, but spun round, thinking she heard her name. Ramón hadn't moved from where she left him, his chest evenly rising with regular breathing. But there was a movement of his lips. She went back. *'Gracias.'*

Hannah exploded. 'You cheat!'

'I know,' he grinned faintly.

'You were asleep earlier?'

'Yes. Come here.' He had still not opened his eyes, but he whispered, 'You have put me to bed without giving me a good night kiss.'

'Behave, Riviero! I'll see you in the morning.'

He lifted one hand—such an elegant hand, but how weakly he lifted it. She saw the red mark where the blood had been drawn off that evening. Full of pity, she took his hand and squeezed it for a moment. 'Now go back to sleep.'

He developed strength suddenly, pulled her down beside him on the bed, moving over to make room for her beside him. She laid her head on his shoulder, his arm close round her. His shoulder was round and smooth and strong and smelt of the man of him. She lay with her cheek against him, not wanting to move, listening to his deep regular breathing. . .

It was dawn when she awoke, still in the same position. She sat up, rubbing her eyes, putting back her hair from her face. This time Ramón was deeply asleep. She smiled down at him in the morning light, then she stole quietly from the room and back to her own. Her dress was very crumpled, her hair tangled. And when she took off her earrings, she found she had lost one. What did an earring matter when you had lost your heart? Hannah threw the dress into the wardrobe and reached for her swimsuit and *pareo*.

She was exhilarated—not at Ramón's strength, but at his weakness—the way he had shown her his exhaustion and dependence. It made her feel strong and happy. But as she ran down the beach, Dolores' warning echoed in her mind—don't get close to him. Perhaps last night was close enough for comfort . . .

Rosita arrived as Hannah was finishing breakfast on the verandah. 'Don't disturb Ramón—he slept here last night,' Hannah told her.

'You spoke with the Brute at San Nicolás?' Rosita's lovely eyes were large with hope.

'Yes, and I met your uncle. He gave me this.' Hannah gave Rosita the list of names. 'I'll leave it with you, Rosita. I'm not part of your campaign, but I'll help, of course, if I can.'

'Thank you, Dr Hannah. You have done much for Ramón.'

'So I'm told.' Hannah smiled to herself. Everyone seemed to think she had been kind—but had she really ever had any choice? This man had strode into her life with all the timidity of a cyclone. She had merely been caught up in its outer rings.

Rosita went into the hospital to see to the patients. When she came back she said, 'Ramón is still asleep. He must have exerted himself very much last night.'

'What do you mean by that?' Hannah turned—only to receive her diamond and emerald earring from the other woman, who gave her a very knowing smile.

'I didn't . . .' Why bother to explain? It might look as though she had made love with Ramón. She looked into Rosita's face. 'You don't mind?'

'I?' The other girl was genuinely surprised. 'I am not Ramón's woman. He sleeps at my mother's house, but he has my brother's room. I am not like that, Dr Hannah.'

'Neither am I, Rosita,' said Hannah quietly.

'Yes, doctor.' Rosita seemed to accept the statement. Hannah was relieved that they had cleared the air. So Ramón had no female companionship. Well, perhaps in his weakened state it was just as well. Yet later that day she saw Ramón with Rosita on the beach. They were walking close together, very slowly, and talking earnestly. Still, it was no business of hers. She would take Dolores' well-meant advice, and keep clear of the handsome Ramón from now on . . .

It was six in the evening when she finally closed the front door. Ramón had not put in an appearance that day, and she was glad. She showered and changed. After yesterday, all she wanted was a simple meal and an early night. She walked down to Pepe's ordered lamb and peppers, drank some wine, and began to relax. It might almost be as it was before Ramón had arrived in San Agustín. Her battered heart began to regain its shape, as she chatted to Pepe. Then Esteban came in, and the conversation turned to cars. 'My friend at the garage has just got one very nice second-hand BMW,' he told Hannah.

'You think it would suit me?'

'You can see.' His eyes lit up.

'Now?'

'Sure. I will telephone to Léon for a test drive.'

Hannah began to think it was a nice idea. 'How powerful an engine? I'm not coming to drive a tank.'

'Only 318,' Estaban told her.

'That sounds OK. Shall we go?'

They drove to Mogan in the twilight in Esteban's little Seat. The used BMW looked brand new, but it was bright red. 'I hadn't wanted red,' said Hannah. 'But why not?'

She said she would give her answer in a couple of days. The little car posed on the forecourt, elegant and proud, just as Hannah had wanted to be. She began to feel a tingle of ownership as they drove away. 'I think it will suit me, Esteban,' she decided.

Esteban lived just outside San Agustín. 'You can drop me here, Esteban. I'd like to walk back—it's a nice night.' She walked along the beach path, enjoying watching the tourists, part of the cheerful scene, yet not part of it.

But when she came in sight of the hospital she saw a group of men on the verandah. Her first thought was to march up to them and order them away. But they weren't villagers; they wore smart clothes, and they were standing grouped about a seated figure in a thre- atening way. The seated figure was Ramón. Hannah waited under the palm trees on the beach path, unwilling to burst in on a private conversation.

Within ten minutes there came the sound of a police

siren. The main station was only yards away from the hospital. The siren seemed to have a curious effect on the men, who seemed to dislike the sound immensely, for they melted away into the darkness, leaving Ramón alone on the verandah. Hannah watched them make for a couple of black Mercedes saloons and drive out on to the highway, once the police car had passed.

Ramón got to his feet as he spotted her coming. 'You saw those men?'

'Yes. Friends of yours?'

'Hm—Some friends! Benito's Mafia.'

She looked up. 'No kidding? How many has he got?'

'They said a hundred, but I don't believe them. Benito is too mean to pay so many. But enough to make life tough for the men who want to strike. He seems to hold all the aces.'

Hannah was silent for a while. Somehow this business was getting more menacing. She felt uncomfortable. She said tentatively, 'Ramón, you must have some shares in your father's businesses.'

'I suppose I must,' he shrugged.

'Can't you find out? You might be able to get support from the other shareholders—do it legitimately, without all this cloak and dagger stuff.'

'I am seeing the company lawyer. I spoke to him today. He's very much the sort of guy to kowtow to the strongest—name of Piedras, Felipe Piedras.'

'Then he'd better find out that you are the strongest, Riviero,' said Hannah firmly. 'Get on the phone again and make it clear.'

He smiled. 'After tonight's visiting delegation that you just saw, I think that is an excellent idea.' And he went in. She heard him on the phone, his voice powerful and lucid. The conversation went on a long time. Hannah left him to it, and went to bed. She kept trying to extricate herself from Ramón's affairs. Maybe the lawyer would do the trick.

She didn't sleep. She heard Ramón go outside again, down the steps. He must be going to Rosita's. Good —now she could switch off completely and get Ramón out of her head.

Suddenly she heard footsteps in her room, and Ramón's voice came in the dark, 'You asleep?'

'No.'

'Felipe sounds OK. He's coming over the day after tomorrow. Where shall I take him for a meal?'

'If you want to impress him, the Rio del Luna,' suggested Hannah.

'Thanks.' She noticed that he had improved his manners lately. He said casually, 'By the way, Hannah, I looked for you, but you'd disappeared. Was it that friend in Mogan?'

He was laughing at her. She said smugly in the dark, 'Yes, it was.'

'Did you enjoy yourself?'

'I had an absolutely wonderful time.'

'Good. Only last time the friend in Mogan was a seagull.'

'Everything's fine now,' she assured him.

'Good, good.' There was silence for a while.

'Are you still there?' asked Hannah.

Ramón said slowly, 'Hannah, I don't think I'll be around much longer.'

Her world fell to pieces. She said, 'Oh.'

'I'll stay till you find someone else.'

'Thanks.' She heard him go out very slowly.

CHAPTER SIX

RAMÓN HAD told her in the darkness, but he said no more about leaving during the daytime. Hannah did not bring up the subject. Nor did she say any more about her friend in Mogan. But she went ahead and agreed to buy the red BMW, asking Juan at the garage to give it a thorough service, and to have it cleaned so that she could pick it up when she was ready.

She watched Ramón as he carried on his routine duties in the hospital each afternoon. They spoke only casually together—yet the thought of not having him around was hurtful to think about. She watched him in theatre, where he was looking businesslike, stitching a cut in the hand of one of the men from the cement factory. Rosita was assisting him, comforting the patient, handing Ramón the needle, the antiseptic liquid and the gauze as he required them. They made a handsome couple, their dark heads exactly the same colour, blue-black in the sunlight. Rosita saw the patient to the door, and Ramón looked up and caught Hannah staring. She coloured, and went quickly away.

He followed her. 'What were you looking at?' His voice was almost teasing her, his lips tending to a smile—so very different from when he first came to work here.

'Just assessing your face,' she told him.

'Assessing?'

'Deciding how much better you look since coming here.'

He shrugged. 'That might be because I feel I am making some progress in my campaign. I'll be seeing Felipe again tomorrow. He is a very bright fellow, and he admits I am right to go on trying.'

Rosita came in. 'There is Chico outside wanting to speak to you,' she told him.

'I am on duty,' Ramón reminded her.

Hannah said, 'I'm doing nothing. I'll take over.'

Rosita said, 'You are kind, Dr Hannah. The men cannot always come at other times, and they want to know when they will find some improvements being made.'

'Not right now, I'm afraid.' Ramón sighed. 'Not right now. They grow impatient because I cannot work miracles here.'

They left the room together, the two handsome Spaniards. Hannah remained professionally cool, trying to accept it as natural that they should work together so closely, both in the clinic and out of it. She sat at the desk and pretended to be making notes. But her thoughts would not wean themselves away from Ramón that afternoon, even in his white coat a devastating magnetic personality. And her thoughts went back to the first night they had met. He had embraced her then. If he ever did so again she would not refuse him. Even if it were only for one night, she felt a longing such as she had never known before. She gazed hard at her notes of the previous morning's patients, and thought of nothing but the physical beauty of her ungracious partner, and of the delights she longed to find out for herself . . .

The phone rang and she took it quickly. 'Yes?'

'Hannah—you are alone? Pablo here.'

'You have the results of his blood test? Yes, Pablo, I'm all alone.' Her voice was unintentionally sad. 'All alone as usual.'

'The blood picture is much the same,' he told her. 'No worse, at least—but I was disappointed to find it is no better. I can't understand it really. He looks so much better.'

Hannah said, 'He is better. Maybe it was the whisky —he did buy one bottle.' She didn't like to tell tales, but Pablo was a consultant, and needed the facts. 'Only the one, Pablo. I saw to that.'

'You are very kind to the ungrateful wretch. I believe he will recover, Hannah, I truly do.'

'You aren't just saying that?'

'No. I have faith, and I am always an optimist.'

'What if he doesn't make it, Pablo? How soon will you

tell him? Do you think he will guess . . . ?'

'Hannah, my friend, we will not talk like that,' said Pablo firmly.

After she had put the phone down, Hannah put her head on her arms and cried. This pest of a surgeon had become the only living thing she could think about. He might not care much for her, but at least he was alive, well, working for his living. If he died, if he became weaker and knew what was coming . . . She could hardly bear it. 'Oh, Riviero, you pig—don't you dare to die!'

She didn't expect him to come back to the clinic that day. But as she locked the front door she heard someone on the verandah. Ramón was there, tidy in cream trousers and a dark green shirt. She said, 'Have you forgotten something?'

He smiled. 'I just came to say hello.'

That wasn't like him—too nice, too cheerful. 'Hello,' said Hannah.

'Will you eat with me tonight? Or are you going to Morgan.'

'To my old maid's fantasy, Riviero? You just don't believe me, do you?'

'I didn't say that exactly, Day. But if he did exist, your eyes would be brighter, and your step lighter.' He shrugged. 'Don't forget, I know women.'

'My step is light, man. You just don't notice, that's all,' she told him.

'So will you eat with me?'

'Yes. We don't eat together very often.'

He nodded. 'Not often enough. But I've got this remnant of a life to sort out first. If I'm granted enough time . . .'

Hannah longed to tell him about his blood test, but he had said he didn't want to know. 'You'll do it,' she assured him.

He didn't seem to hear her. 'Tricky things, lives. They come unbidden, and that's the way they go. I hope there won't be pain . . .'

'Stop it!' Her voice was sharp. He was impinging on her recent thoughts, the thoughts that had made her cry.

'Have you been crying, Day?' Ramón moved closer to look into her face.

'Certainly not. I never cry.'

'Hay fever?'

'I don't know what you mean.'

He didn't answer at once, then he said, 'Go and change. Put your brown dress on.'

'That old thing?'

'Yes—please.'

It was clean. Hannah took it out and pulled it on slowly. She brushed her hair and left it loose on her shoulders. She put on simple brown sandals and a string of pearls. Only then did she look at herself in the mirror and see what Ramón had seen—a white-faced girl with a very lost look and rather red eyes. She took out some powder, and tried to disguise the pink. It was nice of him to ask her out. She must keep the conversation flippant if she could. It was the only way.

He drove along the coast a few kilometres. 'I want you to show me the Rio del Luna—the place you told me to bring Felipe. Do you mind?'

'No, I'd like that. Turn left after the next bend. It's down by Puerto Rico harbour.' He wasn't really taking her out for pleasure, then—only to show him the restaurant. That made her feel safer from her feelings. 'What is he like, this Felipe Piedras? Now that you've spoken more with him?'

'Quite a character. He tells me he likes money, fast cars, women and success.'

'Is he married?'

'Yes. To one of the richest women in Spain.'

'I see.'

'I think his interest in women is purely theoretical,' Ramón confided.

Hannah smiled. 'I wonder how that works. Does he sit and write learned papers about them?' They were joking again, and she felt her heart lighten. They turned off towards Puerto Rico, wound through the small town down to the harbour. She said, 'We can park by the harbour wall and walk to the restaurant. It's just up those steps.'

They walked slowly, almost like tourists themselves, watching the hired boats coming in through the harbour mouth as the sun dipped in the west. A couple of topless sunbathers were collecting their things, as the man came round to fold the umbrellas over the sun-loungers. The air was getting cooler and pleasanter. It was peaceful just to wander.

Ramón stopped and gazed out to sea. 'To think this place was uninhabited fifteen years ago! Just another grey sandy beach.'

'Tell me about it,' invited Hannah.

They sat on boulders looking out to sea, to where the green ocean turned into grey-blue sky at the horizon. 'It was when I admired my father for his enterprise. My mother kept telling me how clever he was to have worked his way up in the world. She loved having nice clothes, big cars. I'll never forget her face when he bought her a diamond necklace.'

'Where is she now?' Hannah asked.

'She left him. I see now she couldn't live with his obsession with money. She sold all her jewels and ran away to the mainland. I'm told she married again. But she died in Seville—never got in touch with us again.'

'That's terribly sad!'

'Benito didn't see it as sad,' said Ramón. 'But if he had changed then—been willing to spend more time with us—things might have been different now.' He looked back to her. 'Incidentally, Felipe tells me I'm not exactly a pauper. I do have shares in the companies. So I can afford to buy you a meal.'

Hannah looked sideways at him, putting back her hair so that she could see him more clearly. 'So you have more say in the running of things than you thought?'

He nodded. 'You know, you look very pretty when the sun is on your hair.'

To hide her rush of emotion at the gentleness in his voice she said, 'So my friend in Mogan says.'

'Ah—the friend. When am I to meet him?'

'Soon, I expect. You're bound to bump into one another.'

Ramón smiled again, still not sure whether to believe

her, and stood up. He reached out to pull her from the rock. 'Come on, Day, show me the place I'm taking Felipe.'

She led him along the harbour wall, past the private moorings as well as those for hire, then up a flight of steps. Ramón followed, saying, 'No prizes for guessing who built this wall, these steps.'

'He must have a monopoly,' said Hannah.

'Near enough.' He caught her at the top, and she noticed that his breathing had improved. Formerly stairs had made him puff, but now he was demonstrably better. They walked along a pretty path lined with hibiscus hedges. The Rio del Luna was set back from the path, with tables both inside and outside, and bright umbrellas.

They chose a corner table inside, where they could see without being conspicuous themselves. 'I hope you enjoy the food, now that I've recommended it,' said Hannah.

Ramón looked at her, his dark eyes teasing. 'You can't cook, can you, Day?'

'Not so that you'd notice. I can scramble eggs.'

'What would happen if you married a society man who expected you to produce dinner parties for all his friends?' he asked.

'Employ a cook.'

'Your friend at Mogan wouldn't mind?'

She teased him, 'Everything I do is right with him.'

'What's his name?'

She was winded. But she rallied very quickly, thinking of her smart little car—'Carlos,' she said quickly.

'Ah, so he really has a name!'

'He has a name, a personality—and a very nice body.' She looked innocently into his eyes. Just then the waiter came up, bending to speak in Ramón's ear.

'You are Dr Riviero?' And when Ramón admitted it, he said, 'I think that I recognise you. I was once employed by your father.'

Ramón looked up ruefully. 'He kicked you out?'

'Yes, for asking for more money. But I soon got a job here—this owner pays very well.'

'I'm glad. I wish more would end up like you. I am trying to change things in San Nicolás.'

'That is what I hear, and I wish you well.'

Ramón ordered swiftly and with taste, and the food was brought to them immediately. They were clearly not tourists, and they received the fullest attention. The lamb was delicious, and Ramón was delighted. 'I used to have it like this when I was a boy, Hannah,' he told her, 'with peppers and garlic and a little paprika. It is very good, no?'

She took more enjoyment from watching him eat so well. 'Very good.' They had ice cream afterwards, with sliced mangoes and papayas. It was a meal she would always remember, sitting with Ramón in harmony, talking gently and in peace.

And then he said, 'I'm glad you really do have a friend. And you have Dolores and Pablo. And the girls—Rosita and Carla.'

'Why the concern?' she enquired.

'No concern. I want you to have friends.'

Hannah sat up rather more proudly. 'I came out here without friends, Riviero. When my folks died, I decided to settle here. It was a gamble, buying the hospital, but I did it. I did it alone. I'm tough, Riviero. Keep your pity for those who need it.'

'I know what you are,' he said quietly. 'Maybe better than you know.'

Hannah said briskly, 'Do you want to talk about your plans?'

He shook his head slowly. 'I think maybe you do not wish to be implicated. Things may go wrong. It is better that I keep my ideas to myself.'

'OK, whatever you say. Talk to Felipe, anyway. I wish you well. And you know I'm here if you want me.'

'If you are not in Mogan with your friend!' Ramón was teasing now, and she tossed her head in reply.

They walked back to the car. A silence between them was easy, like friends who understood one another. They said nothing until they got back to the hospital, then he locked the car, and they walked round the side of the hospital to the verandah. He said suddenly,

'Have you any wine?'

'No.'

'Wait—I'll get some.' She sat down, as he ran lightly along the beach path. He was soon back from Pepe's with a small dark bottle. 'Get me some ice, Day,' he ordered.

'Must you ill-treat your poor liver?' Hannah sighed.

'Bloody doctors—can't stop interfering in people's lives!' Ramón rattled at the closed door into the hospital. 'Well, are you going to get some ice?'

She unlocked the door with a poker face. They went in together, and he took out two large brandy glasses. He filled them with chunks of ice, then he twisted the cork in the bottle. 'Watch, Day—please note that I did not use my teeth.' He poured some of the sweet liqueur over the ice. 'Well, Day? Are you going to drink with me or not? Drink or preach? Which is it?'

'I'll drink—to your health.' Hannah gave him a schoolmistressy sort of look. Outside, they could hear the eternal billows, lashing at the shore, slithering back, and lashing yet again. She smiled suddenly, warmly, '*Salud, mi amigo.*'

His flashing eyes calmer, Ramón smiled down at her. '*Salud, chiquita* (little girl).' He sipped at the drink slowly, his eyes still watching her, wary, alert.

'Go on, get it off your chest, Riviero,' ordered Hannah.

He took another drink before saying what she knew he would be saying, only she had not know when. 'I'm leaving—soon.'

She said pertly, 'Well, don't let it worry you. I managed before you came. I'll manage after you go.'

Ramón was slightly nonplussed. 'You won't miss me?'

She concentrated on the colour of the ice, swishing round the dark Tia Maria like a miniature whirlpool. 'No more than you'll miss me,' she said calmly.

He sat down. 'It isn't that I want to go, but I want to get to know the factory and the plantations—get to know the managers and the men.'

'I'll be too busy to think about you,' she assured him.

'I know. Look, I'll stay another week.'

'The longer you stay, the more patients we get, can't you see that?' Hannah reached out with an uncharacteristic show of friendship and put her hand gently on his arm. 'If you're going, Riviero, there's the door.'

He took a deep breath. Not a sigh—was it? 'OK, I'll be off.'

But he didn't go. He toyed with his glass, poured more liqueur, sipped it, put the glass down again and twisted it. Hannah began to feel the pull of him, the smell of him, the physical attraction that was tearing her apart, made more potent by the drink. She cried out suddenly, 'Oh, get out, Riviero!' and as he stood up, she flung herself against him, trying to hold back her crying. 'Go, damn you, go!'

His arms were round her then, squeezing the breath from her. His glass dropped to the floor and shattered. His kiss was fierce and violent in its demands, strong, sweet and brief. Then he tore himself away, kicked the glass to one side and strode out of the room, out of the back door. Hannah heard his footsteps run down the verandah steps and away in the direction of Rosita . . .

She stood for a second, her mouth numb and sore, then she rushed to her own room, where she shut the door, put the light on, and walked slowly to the basin. In the mirror she saw her lip was bleeding, the tissue around bruised and swollen. She splashed her face with cold water and hung up her dress, then she lay on the bed, her eyes wet with unshed tears. She must remember to tell Raquel to be careful of the broken glass . . . In time, she didn't know how long, she fell into a troubled sleep.

She was woken by someone banging on the outside door. Not an unfamiliar noise—an emergency. She hurriedly pulled on jeans and a tee-shirt, pulling on her white coat over them as she made for the front door. She unbolted it. A man stood there with a teenage boy in his arms. 'My son!' he exclaimed. 'I do not know what is the matter!'

'Put him here.' Hannah was used to thinking quickly. While the patient was laid on the couch, she hastily pulled back her untidy hair into a rubber band and

Capture all the excitement, intrigue and emotion of the busy world of medicine

Take 4 free Doctor/Nurse Romances as your introductory gift from *Mills & Boon*.

The fascinating real-life drama of modern medical life provides the thrilling background to these gripping stories of desire, heartbreak, passion and true love. And to introduce you to this marvellous series, we'll send you 4 Doctor Nurse titles and an exclusive Mills & Boon Tote Bag, absolutely FREE when you complete and return this card.

We'll also reserve a subscription for you to the Mills & Boon Reader Service, which means you'll enjoy:

☆ SIX WONDERFUL NOVELS — sent direct to you every **two** months.

☆ FREE POSTAGE & PACKING — we pay all the extras.

☆ FREE REGULAR NEWSLETTER — packed with competitions, author news and much more. . . .

☆ SPECIAL OFFERS — selected exclusively for our subscribers.

There's no obligation or commitment — you can cancel your subscription at any time. Simply complete and return this card today to receive your free introductory gifts. No stamp is required.

Free Books Certificate

Dear Susan,

Please send me my 4 free Doctor Nurse Romances together with my Mills & Boon tote bag. Please also reserve a special with my Mills & Boon tote bag.

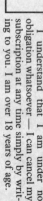

Your exclusive FREE
Mills & Boon Tote Bag

Reader Service subscription for me. If I decide to subscribe, I shall, from the beginning of the month following my free parcel of books, receive 6 superb new titles every two months for just £7.20, post and packing free. If I decide not to subscribe, I shall write to you within 10 days. The free books and Tote Bag will be mine to keep in any case.

I understand that I am under no obligation whatsoever — I can cancel my subscription at any time simply by writing to you. I am over 18 years of age.

Name: _____
(BLOCK CAPITALS PLEASE)

Address: _____

_____ Signature _____

_____ Postode _____ 1A8D

To Susan Welland
Mills & Boon Reader Service
FREEPOST
Croydon
Surrey
CR9 9EL

SEND NO MONEY NOW

NO
STAMP
NEEDED

prepared to examine the boy. Stethoscope round her neck, she first felt the pulse. It was hardly there. She listened to the chest. 'What happened?' she asked. 'Did he just collapse?'

'Yes, doctor. We were just eating—Chinese food at Chou's.'

'Chinese food?' Hannah was alerted then. She looked carefully at the boy's face. Yes, his eyelids were puffy, his lips blue. Allergy. She went quickly to the cupboard for hydrocortisone. 'Don't worry, he'll be all right. Just ring that bell for my assistant, please.' She skilfully injected the vein. 'He isn't used to Chinese food, right?'

'Never tried it before.' The man came back after clanging the bell. 'I took him to my favourite restaurant as a treat, and he enjoyed it very much.'

'Poor chap! He can't take the monosodium glutamate.' Hannah withdrew the syringe very slowly and patted the puncture with a swab, holding it there for a moment to prevent any bleeding. Within a minute the swollen eyelids slowly flickered and opened. 'There —thank goodness!'

The man gazed in admiration. 'You are a very good doctor,' he told her.

Esteban arrived on the run. 'You need an ambulance?'

Hannah said, 'Maybe not. Stand by, Esteban.' She mopped the boy's forehead, felt the wrist again for a pulse. She was suddenly conscious of another figure in the group, and she looked up. It was Ramón. She said briefly, 'Shock—Chinese food. He's getting over it.'

The boy opened his eyes properly, the swelling already going down. 'I am OK,' he muttered.

'Good.' Hannah took his blood pressure again. 'Keep still.'

The man said, 'You will never eat Chinese poison again.'

'But the food was very good.'

Hannah said gently, 'Not for you. Some people can't eat this food—they react to one of the additives. You'll be OK now, I think, but you'd better go home straight to bed.' She beckoned to Esteban. 'Help him.'

Esteban went to help the patient from the couch, where he was already sitting up, his colour better. Suddenly he gasped, paled, and slipped down again. It was Ramón who caught him before he hit the ground. He said hoarsely, 'Arrest! Cardiac arrest. Get some air in his lungs, Day!'

Hannah waited until he was back on the couch, and forced his mouth open. As Ramón began rhythmically squeezing the chest, she breathed a lungful of air into his mouth between thumps. After what seemed like ages, the boy coughed, gasped, then his breathing settled into regular but gasping rhythm. Hannah said briskly, 'I'll go with him to Las Palmas. Get the trolley, Esteban.'

They got him to the ambulance. Hannah phoned Las Palmas, while Ramón and Esteban got the boy settled. Ramón was beside him, his fingers on the pulse. 'I'll go, Day. Get some rest.' His voice was brusque.

She didn't answer, just closed the doors as Esteban started the engine. She stood, watching the van until it was out of sight, then she began to feel how tired she was, and how much her lips hurt. She walked back to the hospital. Rosita Alfonso was there, alerted by the bell. 'Are you all right?' She wanted to know. Then her eyes opened wide. 'Oh, Dr Hannah, your poor mouth!'

Hannah shrugged it off. 'It must have happened in the resuscitation.'

'I can do nothing?'

'No, Rosita. Let's get some sleep.'

The woman left her, with a last concerned look. Hannah realised why when she went back to her room. The bruising was worse. She stood gazing at the marks Ramón had inflicted. The tears ran down her cheeks, as she yearned with all her soul for the man who had made the marks. And she blushed at the same time, ashamed of her own weakness in full view of Rosita.

In the morning she was not in a hurry to open the doors, as there was no queue of patients. She took her time, breakfasting on watermelon and Canary bananas, before going to the front door and unlocking the main doors. The van was back in place by the door, but Esteban had left the back doors of the ambulance swinging open. Hannah went out to close them.

'Good morning, Day.'

Ramón was just getting up, stretching his back as he rose from the stretcher in the van. 'Riviero, you're a fool!' exclaimed Hannah. 'There was more comfortable space in the clinic. Why didn't you come to a comfortable bed?'

'Didn't want to disturb you.'

'Idiot! How was I to know you'd be daft enough to sleep in the van?'

He vaulted lightly from the van and smoothed back his hair. Then he stopped, suddenly seeing the bruising round her mouth, his eyes hurt and guilty. For a moment he faltered, then he put out his right hand and touched her lips with his fingers. Even that gentle touch was painful, and she winced. Ramón said, 'OK, Day, take it easy. I'll get out of your hair.'

The pain inside was even worse than the physical. Hannah said under her breath, 'Here's to our never meeting again.'

Ramón tossed back his hair. 'I'll drink to that.'

She stood as he walked briskly away and got into his car. She waited for the start of his engine. It was a long time coming. But then he ignited, and swerved the little Alfa with a screech of tyres on to the main road to San Nicolás.

Hannah spent a long time that day just cataloguing her own idiocy in falling for a man as unsuitable as Ramón Riviero. Her thoughts went with him, every inch of the road to San Nicolás. She had no excuse. Her own instincts had warned her against him, even before Dolores told her that Latin men only played with foreign women.

She sat on the verandah, looking out at the beach, at the breakers, at the tourists. Was this the vista she wanted to see for the rest of her life? It was clear that meeting Ramón Riviero had been like being involved in an earthquake. From now on, she had to work without him, knowing that she needed him as a baby needs milk.

In love—what a shameful thing to say! Surely an educated woman could control that sort of thing? Superficial attraction she could have coped with, but to be drowned in her own emotions, brought to tears at the very thought of a man—Hannah knew it was so traumatic that she had to start thinking about what to do next. It was almost unthinkable that she could stay here, carry on as though nothing had happened.

She carried on. Two weeks went by. Rosita and Carla were at her side. They saved some lives, cured some diseases. Yet Hannah had lost her fulfilment in her job. And the girls were staunch, ignoring her short temper, her snapped commands, her failure to thank them for helping out. They acted together as a team. There was extra work, now that there was only one doctor, and Hannah was pleased at that. It meant she could work from morning till night, and then sleep deeply, worn out with hard work. But when she woke, in the early hours, she woke with pain in her heart, and more than once, tears on her cheeks. It wasn't as easy as it ought to be, to forget a man like Ramón.

She had hoped that Ramón would think her important enough to contact about his progress towards more democracy in his father's business, but as the days went by with no news, she fought the depression that advanced slowly on her, slowing her steps, making her feelings numb. She didn't matter to Ramón Riviero. A useful aide when he needed her, that was all.

It was Rosita who said casually one day, as she went off duty, 'There is no improvement in life at San Nicolás. My uncle was here at the weekend, and he said there is no change. Ramón is living with his father now. Yet he has done nothing to help us. They say he spends time riding with the widow Juana Lorenzo.'

A picture came to Hannah's mind of a comely, well-made-up woman with a coronet of glossy hair, proudly astride a white mare. It made sense. But her loyalty to Ramón didn't fail. 'He needs time,' she said. 'He hasn't been on Canaria long enough yet. He must get to know his opposition before he makes his move.'

Rosita said, 'I want to believe that. Yet the men are saying he is a Don Quixote, tilting at windmills but doing no harm to the real enemy.'

Hannah felt miserable for Ramón. 'How can they be so cruel?' she sighed.

Rosita said quietly, 'Oh, Dr Hannah, Spanish men can be cruel.'

Hannah said, 'So I've heard from other people.' She thought of phoning Dolores, but such was her depression that she could not face a conversation with the gentle, happy Spanish woman.

It was late on a Friday. The hospital was long closed. Hannah was alone, but so far had no heart to go in search of dinner at Pepe's. She was sitting on her verandah, watching the last of the sunset, the scarlet streaks fading from the now gentle sky. The doors were closed, and she heard the telephone only faintly. She went through to take it. She had long ago given up hope of it being Ramón. 'Hello?' she said.

'Dr Day? This is Benito Riviero.' He was affable, courteous. 'I am giving a special dinner to the best of Canaria society next Saturday, and I hope very much you will come.'

CHAPTER SEVEN

AFTERWARDS Hannah decided that she ought to have refused Benito's invitation. He was a swine, unloved by all, and cultivated only by those who admired his money. She didn't like the man at all, and deeply disapproved of his methods of keeping himself in style. An invitation to dinner from Benito Riviero was only slightly less attractive than a dinner with the Borgias. Yet she had accepted immediately, not even stopping to consult her diary. She had said she was free, and would love to come to dinner . . . And now she wondered what Rosita would think of her for dining with the enemy. Her name would join the list of people who sucked up to Benito. Yet all he had, that had made her accept with such alacrity, was a son called Ramón who would also be at the dinner . . .

Benito had been persuasive, mind you. 'One of my more elegant evenings, with the best of Canaria society coming,' he had told her. 'And I will not allow you to come alone. I will send one of my cars for you.'

Hannah didn't argue; he would only overrule her protests anyway. 'Thank you,' she said.

'I am delighted, *señorita*, delighted. Of course, you know that we dress for dinner?'

She smiled to herself. 'I understand. No shorts or training shoes.'

He didn't see the joke. 'No, *señorita*. Long gowns —gowns with style. I am sure you are a lady of style. I look forward to our meeting.'

Hannah put the phone down, feeling like a traitor. Still, maybe an evening at the Villa Pandora would not be totally wasted. She could meet some of the other directors, perhaps—even question them about Benito's reputation, and see if they all supported his views, or if underneath they secretly felt guilty about him. Yes, that would justify her attendance. She would call it a 'fact-finding mission'.

And then she had to drag out her old suitcase containing clothes she seldom needed from under the bed. She had several evening dresses—but so far her simple life had no need of them. She sat on the floor, surrounded by crumpled chiffon and black tissue paper. As she assessed her capability of being a lady of style, she decided on the dark wine red chiffon. It had a full skirt and no back. She tried it on. More problems—her back was not as tanned as her arms. She would have to spend some of her free time in the next couple of days flat on her stomach on the verandah. This 'lady of style' thing was clearly more cumbersome than she had at first thought.

At least the coming dinner gave her something to think about, something to paper over her broken heart. Whenever she found her thoughts wandering to Ramón's majestic body and brooding dark eyes, to the possibility of a life full of love and passion and adoration . . . then was the time to rush to her bedroom, experiment with make-up, and try on her limited choice of jewels. It was better than nothing for taking her mind away from where it wanted to be.

She began to get ready in the middle of the afternoon that day. She spent a long time in a scented bath, then washed her hair and brushed it till it shone. She wore only silk briefs, gold sandals—and the wine-red dress. She chose small gold hoops for her ears, and she sat for a long time in front of the mirror, tinting her pale eyebrows and lashes tastefully darker, and highlighting her cheeks. She had a light pink lipgloss, that looked quite ravishing with her golden tan.

Benito's car arrived while she was still staring at herself in the mirror, wondering if anyone would recognise her, so different did she look from her usual casual self. She sprayed some Nina Ricci perfume on her neck and wrists, then she opened the front door. The eyes of the chauffeur widened in admiration and he gave a respectful bow, before escorting her deferentially to the long white Mercedes.

The drive to San Nicolás took forty minutes. Hannah sat in the back and sipped at the cold champagne from

the cabinet in front of her. They drove through Mogan,
past Léon's garage. And she smiled to herself as she saw
a scarlet BMW in the back yard. It was a bright colour,
all right. No one could miss her in that—her little
'Carlos'. She turned round for a final look as the
Mercedes rounded the bay and turned away from the
coast towards the mountains.

And then they were at the Villa—the gates for once
wide open at their approach. Hannah was greeted by
Rosita's uncle. She managed to say, 'I suppose there's
been no improvement yet?' The butler raised his sad
eyes as he bowed and showed her through to the gold
drawing room. He was on duty, and not allowed to
converse with Benito's guests.

Benito's plump face showed vast approval of
Hannah's appearance. He was standing with a group of
tuxedoed colleagues and one woman, a bored-looking
lady in yellow, with an aquiline nose and inch-long
diamonds hanging from her aristocratic earlobes.
Hannah was introduced, and as usual at large gather-
ings, forgot all the names as soon as she had greeted the
owners of them.

Ramón was not there. She was monopolised for a
while by one amorous *señor*, who asked her point blank
if she were married or engaged. At her answer, he
decided that all was well for his chances, and first kissing
her hand, he secured a glass of champagne from the
silver tray being carried around by a footman. He was
not a clever man; his conversation was all about his own
prowess as an entrepreneur. Hannah began to hope that
there would be more women than herself and the
aristocrat, who had been introduced as Doña Inés
Piedras.

A tall attractive man had been eyeing Hannah. She
thought he looked slightly more intelligent than her
present companion; he had a slim long face, hair that
was slightly silver at the temples, and lively, amused
eyes. As he took another glass of wine from a passing
footman, he said loudly, 'Benito, it is devilish hot in
here. Let's take our drinks into the garden.'

Benito didn't mind. 'Of course.' He snapped his

fingers, and the footmen carried the trays of glasses and the silver dishes of caviar out through large french windows. It was cooler and quite magnificent in the garden. There was a large paved patio all round a large pool, with an island with a palm tree on it in the middle. Peacocks stood or sat around looking slightly bored. Cockatoos fluttered and squawked in the taller cedars. Macaws and canaries perched in the bushes, chirping and singing. Hannah looked around her, charmed by it all. For a moment she forgot it was ill-gotten money that had built this place. It was enchanting in the twilight, with sparkling blue and green lights in the trees, and the villa itself floodlit. Benito said, 'One does not argue with one's lawyer!' and everyone laughed dutifully.

What was even better, she had escaped from the bore who had been clinging to her, and she found herself next to the attractive man she had noticed—the man Benito had called his lawyer. 'You must be Felipe Piedras,' she said as he stood boldly in front of her, shouldering out the other man.

'And you are Hannah, and quite the most perfect woman I have ever met.'

She laughed. 'What an uninhibited remark—and rather insolent, don't you think?'

'I'm a lawyer, Hannah. I always agree with my clients. But no, here I must say that all I said was the truth—and the truth is not insolent.'

'Not even when it comes from a married man?'

'Nothing to do with it.' His eyes crinkled as he spoke, his eyes probed hers with a knowing charm. Hannah found herself relaxing in his company. 'You have met my wife? She comes from the best family on Canaria.' Hannah shook hands with her. She seemed quite indifferent to the fact that Felipe's arm was round Hannah's waist as he made the introductions.

The conversation around them increased in volume as more champagne and sherry was consumed. But then there was a sudden decrease, and all eyes turned to the french window. Ramón stood there, framed in the lighted window. He wore a white tuxedo, and Hannah felt a rush of emotion as he stood, so tall, so powerful a personality, his black eyes brooding and angry. Felipe said softly, 'Here he comes—the Knight of the Sorrowful Countenance.'

'That's not fair!' Hannah had to stand up for Ramón. 'He's nothing like Don Quixote!' And then she remembered someone else had said he was tilting at windmills . . . She looked at him with pitiful eyes. How were these people to know his two frightful secrets? One, that he intended to mount an attack against his father and all he stood for. And two, that he lived every day with the knowledge that very soon it might all come to an end for him. And then, as Ramón took a step forward into the company and held out a hand to someone closer to him, Hannah gasped. Ramón's left hand held a cane, a black cane. He leaned on it as he walked. 'Oh no!' she gasped.

She lost concentration on what Felipe was saying. She heard a buzz of conversation all around her, and was only really conscious of Ramón, as he made his way slowly through the company, shaking hands, murmuring politenesses, making himself agreeable to these men whom he plotted to take over and rule as his father did—except with justice, fairness and democracy.

He was nearing her, but oh, so slowly! She turned back to Felipe, doing her best to concentrate on his witty analysis of the personality of the board members he represented. Felipe was smiling. 'You see, Hannah, the secret is to agree with everyone, remember everything—and then go away and do what you think is best.'

She couldn't even smile. She sensed something powerful close to her, and when she turned, Ramón was there, his left hand on the cane, his dark eyes thrillingly beautiful, incredibly sad. She turned to face him, leaving a sentence unsaid to her companion. 'Hello, Ramón.'

He looked at her without moving, from under his brows. 'Day—I didn't know you were coming.' He took her hand with stiff formality, and she felt the fingers, the slim wrist she knew as well as her own. His grip was not weak. Yet the cane . . . She dared not mention it.

She said simply, 'I hoped I would see you.'

'I can't think why.'

'Because I care—about you and what you have to do

here. You can't land me in the middle of all your affairs up to the neck, and then expect me to forget all about them, you know. It doesn't work that way.'

'Well, I haven't done anything,' he assured her. 'I—I've been ill.'

'With what?'

'It doesn't matter.'

'Have you seen Pablo?' she asked.

'Of course I have. I don't need a nanny.'

Hannah looked up at that well-known statement, into the deep pools of blackness that were his sad eyes. For a moment they seemed to soften, to begin to lower the defences he had put up against her. She tried to smile, but found that her own eyes were brimming with tears. 'Come off it, Riviero,' she started to say, but couldn't finish the sentence.

Ramón cleared his throat. 'You—you are looking like a princess tonight.'

And then Felipe Piedras interrupted. 'Hey, Ramón, there are only three women here. Don't monopolise the prettiest. You're the host—it isn't manners.' And he put his arm round Hannah and drew her away. She didn't see where Ramón went then, as she was surrounded by men who were taller than her and obstructed her view. But when they went in to dinner, she saw that Ramón was in close conversation with the glamorous woman she had seen riding a white horse. The widow Juana Lorenzo . . .

Felipe stuck to her, making sure he was seated next to Hannah. His own wife and the widow were placed on each side of their fat host. Felipe whispered in her ear, 'Benito always likes to have high-born ladies close. It gives him a feeling of security.'

'You have a fairly wicked sense of humour,' said Hannah, trying not to giggle.

'But there is a dash of the truth behind my joking, isn't there?'

'I admit it. You're an astute man.'

'Thank you. I think I have read you correctly—I am allowed to make you laugh at all the guests except Ramón Riviero? Correct?'

She turned to look into the charming but sardonic face. 'Felipe, there's nothing to make fun of. If there were, I would laugh with you.'

He put his hand over hers. 'My dear, don't waste your finer feelings on Ramón. He is a dear friend, but too dramatic, too serious—the Knight of the Sorrowful Countenance, no less. But I promise not to joke about him if you promise not to fall for him.'

Hannah tried to speak lightly. 'Oh, I promise that. I'm a career woman, I don't intend to fall for anyone. Not for the next fifty years at least.' But under her vivid smiles, her heart wept for the man who was under sentence of death. What a lot of fools, to mock at what they did not understand.

The first two courses were delicious—lobster and then roast pheasant. Then a footman came in with a large silver oval dish on a trolley. He did not serve his master first, but wheeled it round to Hannah. Benito called along the table, 'For you, *señorita*. I have plucked the best of my strawberries—my son insisted. You must take first choice.'

She blushed hotly; she hated to be the centre of attention. She knew Ramón was staring at her under straight brows. She thanked the servant, as he placed strawberries, huge and round and perfect, with some slices of mango and papaya, on her plate, and poured a spoonful of cream on them. She waited until everyone else was served before picking up the fruit with the silver fork, putting it slowly in her mouth. She looked up, once she was satisfied that the attention had dispersed away from her. Ramón was sitting, his own fruit untouched, his gaze burning into hers across the length of the table.

She put down her fork. She could eat nothing else that night. Later, as the replete company made their way back to the floodlit garden for coffee and liqueurs, she sat by the pool, waiting for a suitable moment to make her farewells. She saw Benito coming out and ran to speak to him. 'It's been a wonderful party,' she told him. 'You will forgive me if I make my way back? It's late, and I have quite a way to go.'

He agreed, thanking her for coming, and kissing her

hand effusively. 'I will call the chauffeur,' he said.

And then Felipe Piedras was there, tall and close at her elbow. 'There is no need. Allow me to give you a lift, *señorita.*'

'No, please——' Hannah began.

'It is no trouble. I long to take you.'

'Your wife——'

'She is all right.' Indeed, she was chatting to several men. 'We keep Spanish hours, Hannah—a long siesta in the afternoon, and then awake until dawn. I will return, and she will still be talking, I promise you. She will not notice I am gone.'

He said little as they wound their way round the mountainside back to Mogan. Then, on the steep coast road along the cliffs, he said quietly, 'It is not possible to talk sense at dinner parties, but I do know that Ramón is desperately unhappy about the way the estate is managed. I sympathise—in principle. But at the moment there is little that can be done, you know.'

'He intended to argue with his father,' said Hannah. 'But if he is ill, then what can he do?'

'You are right. My advice is to lie low until you are sure of success. Just complaining to Benito will do nothing but make bad feeling—and the men will be no better off.'

'How many of the directors tonight think as you do?' she asked.

Felipe smiled, that knowing, slightly crooked smile that was more charming than a conventional one. 'You are grilling me as Ramón does! Most of them say they believe in democracy and fair wages when you get them on their own, but together, they are afraid the business will fall to pieces if Benito is replaced as head. It is only human nature, Hannah.'

They had arrived at the hospital. Hannah was pleased that Felipe was an honest man. He might joke about Ramón, but she diagnosed that he would be a true and loyal friend. 'I'm grateful for the lift. It's a long way to come.'

She opened the car door, but Felipe had already run round to let her out. He held the door gallantly and gave her his arm as she got out. But then, as she stood up and turned towards the hospital, he caught her against him, murmuring into her ear, 'Please accept this as a tribute to a beautiful woman.' And he bent and kissed her mouth with an expert touch, warm and pleasant, but without the fire and force that she remembered at Ramón. She drew away. He did not follow her, only saying with his nice smile, 'Good night, *preciosa*. I hope we meet again.'

'So do I. But without the kiss,' she added.

'It is nothing, Hannah. Look upon it as though I had given you a rose.' And she didn't argue. After all, he had driven many kilometres for her. One kiss was perhaps what he said it was—merely a compliment to her, to show her how attractive she was.

She forgot the kiss as she fumbled for her key, because she could hear the telephone ringing and knew it might be an emergency. She ran to answer it, kicking off her gold sandals as she ran. 'Hello?'

'Enjoy the experience of an evening with Felipe Piedras?'

A great exultation filled her body. It was Ramón —and he was jealous! 'Hello, Riviero,' she said calmly. 'What do you want?'

'Is he there with you?'

'No. Why should he be?' She was smiling, thrilling that in spite of his offhand way with her, his attentions to the widow Lorenzo, he still felt he had to ring her. 'He must be halfway back to you by now.'

'Don't tell me he left you in peace! He looked as though he wanted to eat you.'

'He left me in peace,' Hannah assured him. There was a pause, during which she yearned to hold him. She could hear chatter in the background, and the distant squawk of a cockatoo. She said, 'I got the impression that he's a good man—underneath a flippant exterior. He's loyal to you.'

'I know.' Now that his mind was at peace Ramón had little more to say. 'I'll perhaps get a chance to talk when he comes back. Good night.'

'Good night, Ramón.' She couldn't bring herself to

call him by his surname.

She sat in the darkness for a few minutes, then she looked at her watch. Pablo and Dolores didn't go to bed early either. She dialled their number, and Dolores answered. Hannah knew she wouldn't mind the question. 'It was only a chest infection, Hannah.'

'But—but he was using a cane to walk. It must have been a bad one. You should have told me.'

Dolores hesitated. 'You told me you didn't care so much. In fact, you said you wanted him out from under your feet.'

Hannah tried to bluster. 'I wanted him out of the clinic. I can't stand the man to work with. But he is—was—my partner, and naturally—well, of course I want him to be all right. After what you and Pablo have told me about him, I can't just switch off and let him die!'

'Steady, Hannah!' She was a touch hysterical, and Dolores' calming words brought her back to normal. 'Ramón had a chest infection—pneumonia, then. Pablo treated him with antibiotics and he responded quite well. It would have cleared more quickly, only the fool would not go to bed.'

'He's an idiot. How can anyone help him if he won't do what he's told? He's like a headstrong child, who thinks he knows all the answers,' said Hannah worriedly.

'He is insecure about what time is left to him. It is natural.'

'Wise, as usual, Dolores. How was his latest blood test?'

'No change at all.'

Hannah felt a sense of dread. 'Dolores, do you think . . .'

'I'm not saying anything, Hannah. But pray for him.'

She swallowed a sob. 'I'll do that.' She put the phone down. How could she stay here and work normally? It was asking too much, when her heart was so full.

Yet she did just that, working as near to normally as possible for the next weeks. One day Carla came in at the end of a clinic. 'There is a very nice man who wants to speak to you,' she told Hannah.

'Is he ill?'

'I don't think so. He just wants a few words.'

Hannah was intrigued. She said, 'Right, send him in. He can have his few words.' But Felipe Piedras was already in, holding in his hands a bunch of red roses. She had not thought of him again, and certainly had not expected to run into him like this. 'Felipe, this is a surprise!' she exclaimed.

He looked dashing and handsome, in narrow grey trousers and a casual loosely fitting cream silk shirt. His smile was as rakishly charming as she recalled it. 'I had to see you again.' He gave her the roses with a little bow.

'You shouldn't! Please—it isn't right.'

'Don't you like roses?'

'They're beautiful. But——'

'My wife has gone to the south of France with her mother and sister,' Felipe told her. 'They do a season there each year. The in thing, I believe—see-and-be-seen sort of holiday.'

'You're telling me you have an unhappy marriage?' said Hannah drily. 'It won't work, you know.'

'I have a superb marriage. Each of us does exactly as we please. Now, dinner tomorrow night? I want to talk over what progress Ramón is making.'

The final sentence won her over. She did want to talk about Ramón. 'Since you put it like that, I think I can arrange to be free tomorrow night,' she capitulated.

'Wonderful!' Felipe looked very attractive as he stood smiling across the room. She couldn't help smiling back. She did like Felipe. He had a sense of humour, and he wasn't crazy or mixed up about things, merely took life in his stride. She was still in a happy frame of mind as she took the roses and arranged them in a crystal vase. The scent was overpoweringly beautiful in the small hot clinic.

That evening she was just locking up when a small man who looked a bit like a Canarian waiter came up the steps, his olive face pale and sickly. 'Oh, doctor, please can I see Dr Riviero? I have bad pains, and he told me next time I have pains I must come and have an operation.'

'Come on. Where's the pain?' Hannah examined him thoroughly. The diagnosis was in no doubt. He had gall bladder pathology—probably a stone. He was in a lot of pain. She gave him an injection to help the pain as she explained, 'Dr Riviero doesn't work here any more. I understand he's thinking of going part-time to Las Palmas . . .'

The man interrupted her. 'No! I cannot go there. Dr Riviero promised—truly, doctor. He promised I do not need to go to Las Palmas.'

Hannah looked round. Rosita was still there, putting things away. Hannah said, 'I shall have to admit this man. He isn't well enough to send home.'

Rosita nodded. 'I will take him to the ward.'

'Do you know if Ramón has started at Las Palmas yet?'

'He has started, yes, but I do not know how many days a week.'

'I shall have to get in touch with him. Have you heard if he's well?'

Rosita nodded. 'He has recovered from his pneumonia.' She helped the patient from the couch. 'Why do you not telephone the Villa? If he has promised to do this operation, then he is a man of his word.'

'I don't like to bother him,' explained Hannah. 'He has so much to think about.'

Rosita was less than charitable. 'That is all he does—think! Never does he do anything—all the time think, think, think!'

When she came back, having settled the patient and given his something to eat, Hannah said, 'I thought you admired Ramón very much.'

'I think he is well-meaning but useless. It is you who are in love with him.'

Hannah felt very vulnerable. 'No, Rosita, I worry about him as a—as—a colleague, that's all.'

The girl looked sympathetic. 'There is no harm in loving.'

Hannah blushed. The girl had found that earring in Ramón's bed. She had also seen the bruises on Hannah's mouth. There was hardly any point in explaining; that would probably make things worse. She said, 'Would you phone the Villa for me?'

Rosita smiled. 'He will wonder why you send me. I cannot describe the symptoms of the patient, Dr Hannah. Better that you do it yourself.'

Hannah knew the number of the Villa off by heart, but she knew she shrank from speaking to Ramón. He had cut himself off from her. He would think she was chasing him, telephoning him like this at home. Her fingers shook as she dialled. 'This is Dr Day. Is it possible to speak to Dr Ramón Riviero?'

In a few minutes, during which she imagined the cool panelled corridor of the Villa, the elegant lounge, she heard footsteps, and the receiver was picked up. 'Riviero?'

'It's Hannah.' And she spoke again quickly, giving him no time to reply. 'I have a man here, Señor Alberto —he tells me you promised to operate on his gall bladder.'

'Oh, hell!' exclaimed Ramón.

'I'll send him to Las Palmas.'

'No, no, don't do that. Poor chap, I remember now. His wife died while on the operating table for varicose veins in Las Palmas. No one's fault, just a sad accident. He's terrified of going to the same place.' He paused. 'Have you admitted him?'

'Yes. He's in a bad way. A lot of pain and guarding.'

'He ought to have it out. When are you free to anaesthetise?'

'Well—now, but that's too rushed for you,' said Hannah. 'How about tomorrow at six?'

'I'll be there.'

She replaced the receiver. Ramón had made it clear that he didn't really want to renew the acquaintance. But his duty to his patient came first. She went to the ward to tell Señor Alberto that Ramón would do his cholecystetomy. The man's relief and joy was painfully obvious. She left him watching television, clutching his tummy but with a smile on his lips.

He was duly pre-medicated at five next afternoon. Ramón had not arrived, but the theatre and both nurses were on duty. Hannah walked about aimlessly, trying to think of something to do, but it was useless. She ended up standing blatantly at the door, watching each car as it rounded the bend from Mogan, to see if it belonged to Ramón.

She saw it far away, a dot on the winding road on the side of the cliff. Her heart went out to him, to his sense of duty, to his responsibility in keeping a promise. He got lightly out of the Alfa. He had discarded his cane, then. He walked up the dusty path—as he had on that first day—long strides, kicking at the odd pebble. Hannah made no attempt to disguise the fact that she was waiting for him. 'We appreciate this, Riviero,' she told him.

He looked down at her, and lost his distant look. 'I remember the case. He wasn't too bad last time I saw him, and I told him to keep off fats.' Hannah kept her composure at his closeness—a physician, she was, welcoming a visiting surgeon. He said suddenly, 'No strawberries today?' He too had recalled that first meeting, then.

She managed a distant smile. 'Not with a prepped patient waiting.'

'Right, then we'd better do some cutting.'

They walked along the corridor, Hannah just in front. She said nervously, 'You—are keeping well, Ramón?'

'There's no need to talk about my health,' he snapped. Then in a softer voice he said, 'I'm fine. I do two days a week at Las Palmas. That I can stand. The rest of the time I try to instil a conscience in my father. Now that is a strain.'

'Is Felipe any help?'

'Moral support only so far. He is very apprehensive about a strike.' Rosita and Carla came out of the ward, and Ramón could only say, 'You haven't seen the old rogue yourself?'

'Felipe? Only in passing.' There was no need to tell him they had a date.

As Ramón scrubbed, the gold chain dangling on the naked chest, he said so that everyone could hear, 'The men are beginning to think I do not care.'

Rosita protested, 'Oh no, Ramón—only that you do

nothing. They know you care.'

She helped him on with his gown and gloves. 'Tell them, Rosita, that I can work better for them if I stay friendly with the Brute,' he said. 'If he kicks me out, I can do even less.'

'Yes, I know that, Ramón. Dr Hannah tells me not to lose faith in you.'

Ramón shot a swift glance at both women under his eyebrows, before reaching for the strings to his mask. 'Shall we start?' he said.

Hannah injected the vein. They wheeled the patient in, and Ramón felt the hypogastrium carefully before arranging the covers around the area. He made his incision, and went on, operating with his usual speed and deftness. No one would ever know he had been seriously ill—perhaps still was. Hannah monitored the patient's breathing and blood pressure. In between she cast longing glances at Ramón, praying that he would not rush away as soon as it was over, but stay and chat to them.

He took a quick look at her over his mask as he began to snip, stemming the bleeding with clamps as each blood vessel was cut. 'So, life goes on here OK?'

'Just the same,' she answered.

'You haven't looked for anyone else?'

'I prefer to be alone.'

The gall bladder was severed, and placed in the small dish Carla held out. As he tidied up the stump and sutured what was left, Ramón said casually, 'It is relaxing to work here. You all work so well together—a perfect team.'

And it was Rosita who said warmly, 'That is because of Dr Hannah. A team always depends on its leader.'

Ramón made no comment. 'Sutures, please.' He was stitching the skin. No one said any more until the last silk was cut. 'Right, stop the gas.'

Hannah withdrew the tube. The nurses took over then, monitoring the heart and blood pressure, tidying his gown, and taking him back to the ward to keep an eye on him. Hannah and Ramón went to remove their theatre clothes. He took a deep breath as he buttoned his shirt, tucked it into his trousers, and smoothed back his hair, as he had a hundred times before. 'Like old times,' he commented.

'A bit. We aren't arguing, though. We used to argue, if you recall.'

'Quarrel? Us? Surely not.'

There was a frank exchange of looks then, a hint of a smile from both of them. He went on, 'What a snob I was, despising this sort of work. I think my heart was still in India—with my manners—when I used to tell you what you did was worthless. I do hope you have forgiven me.'

'You find that India gets on without you?' He was fingering his amethyst on its gold chain, before he pushed it inside his shirt. Hannah felt her cheeks redden as she remembered the night she had slept in his arms. The mark of that amethyst had been pressed deep in her breast.

'She does, God bless her. There are always others ready and waiting to go on with the work. There will always be others. No one is indispensable.'

She said, not expecting any assent, 'Come and have a drink on the verandah.'

'All right, I'd love a beer. It's pretty hot in theatre. No air-conditioning like they have in Las Palmas.'

They went out into the deepening dusk. Hannah brought two beers from the fridge, and as Ramón sat in his usual chair, she stood close to him as she poured the drinks into glasses. For one second she felt his arm round her waist, his face against her chest. Then he took the glass, and the single sweet moment had gone.

She sat opposite him, trying to think of something to say—some small talk that would hide her depth of feeling to be sitting opposite to him again. But there was no point really in trying to get him to stay; he had made it clear that he had nothing more to do here. These few minutes were all she had left.

After a long silence, during which he drank his beer and looked out at the waves, which were noisy tonight, Ramón said, 'You made a hit with my father. He is already planning to invite you again.'

Her heart quickened. So she was still in contact—if

only vaguely—with Ramón. 'I thought he only invited people who are useful to him,' she remarked.

He gave a rueful smile. 'I'm sorry to be sexist, Day, but you were very useful—you were decorative and good to look at, thus making the evening more attractive for the men there.'

'How absolutely—well, sexist!' But her indignation turned to a giggle. 'Gosh, Riviero, you've changed. You would have thought it perfectly acceptable before. Now you can see how women are treated.'

At that moment footsteps were heard coming at a run up the beach path, and out of the darkness came Felipe Piedras, dressed smartly, and carrying a bunch of red roses. Ramón was on his feet at once. Coldly he said, 'I didn't know you had a date.'

Hannah had forgotten completely. Felipe was not in the least perturbed, however. With a low bow he put the flowers into Hannah's hand. 'For the loveliest creature in the world.' Then he beamed at Ramón. 'What are you doing back here? I can't have a rival for Hannah's affections—certainly not a good-looking devil like you.'

Ramón shook his head, but his words were addressed to Hannah. 'I do see how women are treated.' His eyes were hodded. 'Don't let him break your heart, Day. You know he hasn't got one—nor a conscience either.'

She looked at him unhappily, lost for words. Felipe winked at Hannah, but she was looking at Ramón. For a second his eyes bored into hers, then he swung round and walked lightly along the side of the hospital towards his car. Hannah watched him as he merged into the shadows of the scrub and cacti at the front. She heard his engine start, then the noise of the car was drowned by the crashing of the breakers on the beach. A tear rolled down one cheek.

CHAPTER EIGHT

HANNAH stood in the Canarian evening, the breakers wild on the shore, the wind stirring her hair. Felipe Piedras moved towards her and stood beside her, not touching. 'You won't want to come out now.' It was a statement, not a question. 'You looked at each other, Hannah—and there was something between you that shut out the rest of the world.'

She was moved by his perception, but she didn't intend to confide in him. 'Something between us? Nonsense! Don't you think he would have stayed if there was? It was his decision to leave, you know. I didn't fire him.'

'You look so sad, Hannah dear. Do I take you out and cheer you up with my wit and charm, or do I tactfully leave you to grieve in peace?'

She looked at him gratefully. 'You're good company, Felipe. But I'm afraid you'd waste your evening. I have nothing to give you in return, either mentally or physically.'

'You will not sleep with me, then. OK—I can live with that,' he shrugged.

She smiled. Felipe sat down in the chair vacated by Ramón. She said, 'You mean you don't mind?'

'Hannah, my name is Felipe Piedras, not Don Juan. I can have plenty of women for that. I treat you as a valued friend.'

'Oh, that does sound lovely. I'd accept your invitation, then—if I didn't think it was only another of your lines that you keep for women who are used to the old ones.'

He chuckled, enjoying the mental sparring. 'Ever suspicious, *preciosa*. Come with me. That is the only way to find out.'

Hannah made up her mind. 'I will. And thank you. Will you give me ten minutes to shower? We had a late

119

operation, and I forgot to phone and warn you.'

'I will wait all night for you, my angel.'

She got ready quickly, not really sure if she was being wise. Yet why not? They were on the same wavelength, she and Felipe; she thought they could spend an evening together without becoming involved. She wound her hair up in a coil, and wore a simple cotton skirt and thin white blouse, then went back to the verandah. 'I'm sorry, Felipe, I ought to have offered you a drink.'

'You had enough on your mind, my angel.' He was so gentle, so very un-neurotic. 'You are ready? Come, we will go in search of champagne.'

'Don't spoil me!' laughed Hannah. 'I'll pay my way.'

'Ah now, we Latin men can't take kindly to that,' Felipe protested.

'Oh, but you must. Otherwise I shall have to cook a meal for you in exchange—and my cooking is diabolical!' Laughing, he steered her down the steps and along to his Mercedes, parked in the tourists' car park behind Pepe's. It was such a relief to be with someone intelligent and relaxing and funny. Hannah began to feel good. Ramón would have been darkly disturbing, wrapped up as he was with his conscience, his duty, that wouldn't let him rest.

All the same, she wanted to talk about him. 'What are you going to do for Ramón?' she asked.

'What I can. Benito Riviero is my employer at the moment, and apart from being made of jelly on the outside, he is hard cruel steel at his centre.'

'And you support Benito against Ramón? You are on the winner's side?'

'Of course. My firm is in business to make money.'

'Benito could have said that, Felipe. You disappoint me.'

'Then I will add to it—to make money, and to stand for justice as far as possible under the circumstances.'

'It's strange,' mused Hannah, 'you are Ramón's opposite—yet he likes you.'

'We respect each other's intellect and honesty.' He looked down at her in the shadowy car park. 'And we both adore you.'

'Don't talk like that!'

'I saw how he needs to be near you.' His dark eyes were serious. 'It seemed to be a physical need for him.'

'Don't—please don't.' And he saw how he had distressed her. Immediately he changed the subject. They drove along the coast road, and he told her of his student days in America, where he had studied at Harvard. He had thought he would never settle again in such a small place as San Agustín—yet here he was, with a large villa and three cars, happy as he could be anywhere. Hannah listened, fascinated by his life story, by his character, so level-headed and sane, so ironically amused by human frailty and weakness.

He drew up in Mogan, and she looked round her, surprised. She had not noticed where they were heading. 'We will eat seafood and drink champagne. There is a small café on the hill, with a view of the harbour.' They climbed up some steps, flanked on each side by bushes of luxurious flowering plants that smelt heavenly. Felipe was welcomed by the proprietor as a dear and valued client. Their table was out on a balcony, and the view across the lights of Mogan was beautiful. Out at sea they could see a few fishermen's boats. The meal was superb, the champagne came in a large bottle, and Hannah's head was swimming as they descended the steps.

She thought he would be driving her home, but instead, they walked down to the harbour. 'You will enjoy a moonlit cruise.' Felipe had stopped by a neat blue and white yacht. Her name was *Titania*.

'This is yours?' queried Hannah.

'Of course. What else would I do without a hobby, with my wife off with her mother whenever Monaco society demands her?'

Excited, Hannah climbed on board. Felipe handled the boat neatly, starting the engine to manoeuvre her out of the harbour. Once outside the harbour walls, in a gentle swell, he cut the engine to minimum and they floated gently towards the horizon. Felipe said, 'Well?'

The shore looked magic from here, with twinkling lights all the way up the cliffs. They could hear nothing now but the sound of the water lapping against the sides of the boat. Hannah found herself in Felipe's embrace without trepidation. He held her gently, as though she might break, with apparently no thought of passion or of possession.

Then he kissed her gently on the forehead. She was not afraid or annoyed. When he kissed her mouth, he did it so softly that it made no impression, like the light winds that floated over them, making no impression on the boat. When he took her face in both hands and kissed her with open mouth, she was so lulled by the champagne and by the easy way he had led up to it, the trusting attitude she had developed, that she felt only pleasure, fulfilment of a physical need.

It was some time later that she came to her senses and realised where she was. 'What is it, darling?' he asked softly.

'Enough.'

'You are enjoying yourself. Come back to my empty arms.'

'If I do, then we can't be friends any more.'

'We can. We are both intelligent people. Hannah, there is no harm in a little loving.'

'There is to me.' She looked unhappy. 'I couldn't trust you again—and I want to go on liking you.'

He laughed at that, and ruffled her hair, which was already extremely untidy, the pins lost for ever. 'I understand you, *preciosa*. And I don't want that to happen.' He allowed her to stand up and straighten her blouse. 'I want to take you out again tomorrow. And the next day. And the day after that.'

She smiled down at him in the darkness, as he sat with his back against the deckhouse. 'Come now, Don Juan, make someone else's day. Don't allow one woman to monopolise you.'

He started the engine. 'Come here, help me steer.' They stood together. His hand went round her neck, down inside her blouse, his fingers warm and still against her breast but she moved gently away.

'Put both hands on the wheel,' she told him. 'We're coming in close, and we need an experienced man to bring us in.'

'And you think I am an experienced man? Perhaps you are right.' His chuckle was disarming in the darkness. Hannah felt safe, comfortable, so nice had he been with her.

They drove back along the cliff road to San Agustín. It was deserted so late, and Felipe drove fast, humming to himself, satisfied with his outing. He was looking sideways at Hannah. 'You enjoyed it as much as I did, *preciosa*?' Then suddenly the front wheel struck a rock that had fallen on the road and the car veered out of control. Then it broke through the crash barrier on the cliffside and tumbled sickeningly over on to the roof. The cliff was not steep there, and they stopped after it had slipped another few feet down the stony path and turned again the right way up. They were both strapped in, but Hannah had knocked her face against the side window. The engine stopped, and they were alone in a sudden eerie silence.

'My darling, are you all right?' demanded Felipe frantically.

'I think so.' She put up her hand to feel the graze on her cheekbone, and felt the wetness of blood. Foolishly she worried about it staining her blouse. 'Are you all right, Felipe?'

'I am. Now I must figure out how to get back on the road.' He opened the car door, and reached for a torch in the glove compartment. 'Come, darling, sit on this flat rock while I check to see if I can drive back without slipping.' He helped her to the rock.

She sat, feeling shaky, glad things were no worse. 'You will come back for me when you get to the top?' She tried to joke, to show she was all right.

'Don't worry, I wouldn't leave you here to get a lift from the morning cement lorries. You are too precious to me.' His voice had regained some of its cheery optimism. 'I won't be five minutes.'

Hannah sat on the rock, but something seemed to be happening to the lights ahead—they kept moving, and blurring in front of her eyes. She didn't realise she was slipping to the ground, only that something sharp was sticking into her back . . .

And then it was morning. Blinding morning sunshine was streaming in through an unfamiliar window. She was in a hospital bed—so much was obvious. She put up a hand to feel a dressing on her cheek. It hurt, stung badly under the dressing. And her head ached all over, a throbbing, banging pain.

A young nurse popped her head in. Seeing Hannah awake, she went across to her. 'You are feeling better?'

'Under the circumstances. Is it concussion? I feel as though my head is inside a cement mixer wrapped in cotton wool!'

The little nurse laughed. 'I'll bring Sister Rodriguez. She wanted to know as soon as you came round.' So Dolores was here. It must be Las Palmas hospital, Santa Teresa's, where Pablo and Dolores worked. The nurse's skirt rustled as she went away and Hannah leaned back on soft pillows. She felt as though she were drifting, swimming . . . her back ached as well as her head. It was such a nice day to stay in bed for a while. Just to sleep—just to sleep . . .

'Hannah, what a shock you gave us!' Dolores was at her side. 'I was on duty when the stretcher came in. How do you feel?'

'Thirsty. And concussed.'

'You are badly bruised, but nothing is broken, thank God.'

Hannah was suddenly puzzled. She couldn't remember what had happened. 'Dolores, was I with someone last night?' she asked.

Her friend's face looked concerned. 'You don't remember his name?'

Hannah thought hard, and her head ached more. 'No—it's all blank. Oh, Dolores, please tell me what happened?'

'I can't, dear. But the man you were with is all right. They kept him in overnight, but he is going home today.' She paused. 'Does the name Piedras mean anything?'

'Piedras?' It meant nothing. 'Piedras who?'

'Don't worry, Hannah. Just rest and get over it. I'll stay with you. It will come back in time. I'll get you some tea—but no solids today.'

'Why does my back hurt so much?' Hannah wanted to know. 'Did I bruise it?'

'No, dear. You fell on a broken wing mirror and there is some glass in the wound. You will be going to surgery later today. Ramón will operate.'

'Ramón?' Hannah wondered why Dolores said it as though she knew a Ramón.

'Ramón Riviero. Oh, Hannah, how can you know me, yet not remember Ramón?'

'I think I know the name—a little,' Hannah said vaguely. 'It was a long time ago?'

'You mustn't try to remember,' said Dolores. 'It will all come back soon. Sleep now.'

Hannah slept fitfully all day. She knew that the sun moved from one side of the room to the other, but she could not recall the events of last night. And the name Ramón kept coming back, but there was no face that came with the name. Pablo Rodriguez came to see her; she remembered his plump shape and happy smile. But there was a white-coated *medico* with him. Hannah was too sleepy to take much notice, but she liked his face, although she had never seen him before.

When she opened her eyes again, the strange doctor was sitting on the bed. She struggled to focus her eyes on the handsome face. He was alone. This must be the surgeon who was going to operate on her; Dolores had mentioned it. But why was his brow so creased and anxious-looking? Why were they alone, without a nurse with him, as regulations required? He seemed to be struggling with his emotions. As her eyes opened again, she saw him brush away tears from his very dark eyes with a slim brown hand. She liked his hands, they looked capable and elegant. She smiled up at him and he said hoarsely, 'You don't know me?'

'No.'

'You recognised Dolores and Pablo. Why don't you know me? I am their friend.'

'Then maybe we met at their place?' Hannah suggested.

He shook his head sadly. 'Don't try to remember. Rest now. I'll be operating in about an hour to get the glass from your spine.'

He went out, and the little nurse came in. 'I've brought your pre-med, and operation gown. Isn't he handsome? He's our new consultant—only part-time, because he hasn't been well. But you are very lucky. He usually only operates twick a week, but he has come in specially to do yours. Maybe it's because you are a doctor yourself? You get special treatment.'

'I don't want special treatment,' said Hannah firmly.

The surgeon came back while the nurse was getting Hannah ready. 'Don't forget a clean dressing on the face, nurse,' he ordered.

'No, sir.'

He came to the bed again. 'You feel OK?'

'My head aches,' Hannah told him.

'I know. I'd thought of leaving the operation until tomorrow. But there is a lot of splintered glass in there and it might move inside the spine, then it might cause trouble.'

'Thank you for explaining,' said Hannah. 'I don't mind, but I wish I knew how the glass got there.'

'It was a car accident. You were on the Mogan road—or rather off it. You were a passenger in Felipe Piedras' Mercedes.'

'Felipe Piedras . . . Mercedes . . .' Hannah felt perplexed. It was too much trouble to think.

The surgeon said briefly, 'I'll talk to you after the op.'

'Fine.'

She was wheeled along a cool corridor. Air-conditioning. Who had told her that Santa Teresa's was air-conditioned? The combination of concussion and her pre-med made her feel very pleasantly drowsy. In the theatre she was aware of several gowned and masked figures, talking about her. 'Safer with a local.' A needle was inserted in her back—only a prick. She was turned almost on her stomach, and wedged with pillows. The handsome surgeon asked if she were comfortable. She knew who it was, because he had such a nice voice. She knew they were fiddling with her back. She heard the clink of instruments on the tray. She slept through the rest of the operation.

When she woke, it was morning again. Her body ached, but her head was clearer and the concussion was gone. The little nurse came in. 'Good morning, Dr Day—would you like some breakfast?'

The other Sister came in as she was eating cereal. 'How is your memory today, doctor?' she asked.

'Memory?' echoed Hannah. 'Have I forgotten something?'

The Sister helped her to sit up, brought her another pillow. 'Do you know why you are in hospital?' she asked.

'I needed some glass removed from my spine. Was it successful?'

'We think so. You have the best surgeon in the country.'

'I did? He was very kind . . .'

'He was insistent that no one else be allowed to operate.'

Later that day Pablo and Dolores came together to see her. She felt well, only a little uncomfortable. They joked about her lying in comfort while they worked, but when they asked about the accident, Hannah only shook her head wanly. 'It's too soon, Dolores, it's too soon.'

Some red roses arrived for her—from someone called Felipe. Someone called Ramón came in, wearing a white coat, and sat with her for a while. He carried no flowers, but his face was nice, his eyes very deep and thoughtful.

Then, in the evening, Carla and Rosita came to visit. Their eyes showed signs of weeping. Hannah greeted them happily, glad she recognised them, that her memory had not failed her completely. 'So the hospital at San Agustín is empty?' she asked.

'We have put up a notice,' they told her. 'Dr Arora will see patients for us.'

'That's good. I think I'm going to need a couple of weeks to convalesce.'

Rosita said, 'Sister said you have forgotten Ramón.'

'Not forgotten—not completely. I know the name.'

But her face must have been troubled, because Sister didn't allow the visit to go on any longer. 'You can come again tomorrow,' she told the nurses.

It was late that evening, when the shadows from the setting sun had long gone, and the lights were on in Santa Teresa's Hospital, that the man they called Ramón came again, alone, and stood for a long time by the door. He wore no white coat this time, but Hannah would have recognised that upright figure and brooding face anywhere. When he didn't move, she said brightly, 'Please come in. I want to thank you for what you've done for me.'

He sat down. His voice was pleasant, gentle. 'You have a very selective amnesia, Hannah. Is it only people who have hurt you deeply that you refuse to remember?'

'Hurt? I've never been hurt, Doctor.'

'Mentally?'

'Mentally I feel cheerful. No hang-ups, if that's what you mean.'

'No—no—painful memories—about any man?'

Hannah laughed. 'No, Doctor. No boyfriend and no painful memories. I wouldn't forget if I had a man I loved.'

'Perhaps you would if—if your experiences of him were painful.'

Hannah's reply was emphatic. 'Truly there's no one. I live alone, and that's how I like it. I don't wish to be involved—it's too much trouble.'

'That is what I feared,' he sighed. 'You have told me what I wanted to know.'

'I have?'

'That Riviero and Piedras are names too painful for you—too much trouble.'

'If you say so. Please tell me who they are?'

'I am Riviero,' said Ramón.

'You can't be.' Hannah was puzzled suddenly. 'No, he's in India, Doctor. He's a good man—he works in poor countries, where they have no hope.'

The surgeon's face twisted, and he turned his face away. 'You have some recollection, then?' He stood up and walked to the window, looked out on to the dark hospital gardens.

Hannah tried very hard. Riviero, Riviero . . . Then she said faintly, 'A gold chain. An amethyst . . .' The man at the window turned and came to the bed. He sat down and reached inside his open-necked shirt, pulling out a bright gold chain, with a large purple amethyst set in gold, dangling at the end of it. 'Yes—like that.' Her eyes filled suddenly, and she closed them, feeling tears coming. 'Yes,' she whispered, 'I remember the amethyst . . . And bruises—bruises on my mouth . . .' She lay for a moment, eyes tightly shut, as memory after painful memory flooded back, feeling the exquisite agony of her obsession with Ramón Riviero, of her misery when he left her, and her trying to forget him by going out with Felipe Piedras . . . 'I do remember, Ramón.'

When she opened her eyes, he was standing at the window, putting the jewel back inside his white shirt. He turned round slowly, and their eyes met in full understanding. He said, 'I'm glad you have remembered. You will soon be better now.' He came closer to the bed, and she saw the black eyes that she loved. 'I am sorry my name is painful to you, Hannah. I hope the pain will soon pass.'

'Don't go yet.' But he reached out a hand and touched hers briefly, then went swiftly from the room. Hannah turned her face to the wall and wept. The pain was bad now—not the operation scar, but the pain in her heart. And he must know now how deeply she loved him. He had made his escape very quickly—making it all too clear that he wanted nothing to do with Hannah Day's finer feelings.

She lay in bed, getting stronger. On the seventh day Dolores came to take the stitches out. 'You are looking better for the rest, Hannah,' she said. 'I think you should come to my house for a week, and not have to look after yourself.'

'You're kind, but I want to go back, truly. I won't open the hospital right away, but I'd like to be back among my own things. Pepe can bring me food.'

The last stitch came out neatly. 'Does it hurt?' Dolores drenched the wound with iodine, and put a clean dry dressing lightly over it. 'Ramón must see this before you can be discharged.'

'He doesn't stay long, does he?' remarked Hannah.

'Hardly comes into the room but he's out of it again.'

'He feels that his presence does you no good.'

'I could have told you that.' Hannah sighed. 'The pest! One look at those eyes, and I wonder if he'll ever smile again.'

'That is why Pablo got him here to work. It was bad for him to sit brooding at home, powerless to do anything against his father.'

Hannah said, 'I guess he can't stand my guts, or he could have stayed at San Agustín. I suppose it must be awful knowing your employer is falling for you.'

Dolores looked worried. 'You aren't, are you? You told me——'

'Of course. Don't worry, Dolores. And thank you—you've been so wonderful to me.'

'I am going to insist that you stay with us for at least a couple of days,' said Dolores. 'I have to be sure you don't do too much.'

'All right, just for a day or two. I'm hungry, and the thought of your cooking is too tempting.'

'Hungry? What an excellent sign! Pablo will bring you in the car when Ramón has given you the all-clear.' Dolores bent and kissed her, then she went to the door.

'Dolores——' Hannah began.

Her friend looked back, her hand on the handle. 'What now?'

'Don't invite Ramón too. The less I see of him the better.'

Dolores laughed. 'I'll try and keep you apart!'

But Hannah's laughter died as soon as the door was closed. She had to face two weeks' convalescence—two weeks of doing nothing, with only her sad thoughts to live with. She couldn't imagine the hospital at San Agustín all alone with nothing to do. Empty—empty and echoing, the corridors silent, the windows closed to keep out the sound of the waves . . .

The door opened and she gathered her thoughts quickly. Ramón Riviero came in—alone as usual, his white coat flapping open. 'How is the back?' he asked.

Hannah was herself again. She looked up from her comfortable position on the pillows and said pertly,

'Shouldn't you have a Sister with you when you visit a lady patient?'

He looked down, a hint of a smile touching his lips. 'I should. Now turn over.'

'You have a cheek, Riviero! You think the rules are there only for other people to obey.'

'Something like that. Turn over when you are told, woman.'

'Are you going to help me?' asked Hannah invitingly.

'No, of course not. I want to see how you manage by yourself.'

'Pig! *Cerdo*.' She turned over on to her tummy, quite easily. The wound had healed well.

Ramón pulled the thin nightdress up and she felt him lift the dressing from the wound where Dolores had put it. He touched the skin around the incision. 'That is really an excellent scar,' he told her.

'That's because I have excellent healing properties.'

To her astonishment, his hand moved down and smacked her sharply on the behind, before pulling her gown demurely back into place. She turned over, half laughing, her indignation turning into giggles. Ramón said, 'It is an excellent scar entirely due to the fact that you were lucky enough to have the best surgeon on the island.' As their laughter died, he went on quietly, 'And thank God it was no worse. You don't have to tell me this, but was Felipe drunk that night? Was he fooling with you in the car?'

'No, neither of us was drunk, and we weren't fooling. I think he was just showing off a bit—the road was quiet, it's a lovely car, and he's a good driver. He was just going too fast, and some rocks had fallen from the cliffs into the road.'

Ramón breathed out a long sigh. 'I have not known Felipe be so reckless.'

'It's over,' said Hannah. 'Forget it.'

He looked down at her. 'Will you ever go with him again?'

'A married man isn't the most sensible escort. If the papers wanted to, they could have made it into a sensation—that we were drunk, or having an affair.'

'And that isn't so?'

'Riviero, you know us both better than that!' retorted Hannah.

He gave a slight smile, as though still not sure. 'Maybe.'

'Oh, come on, Riviero. You know what a pillar of society I am.'

'Pillars of society are usually older and uglier than you.'

They exchanged a long look. There seemed to be more in his eyes than Hannah could read. Then he stood up. 'You can go home if you like. See you, Day.'

'Yes. I'll see you at Benito's dinner party.'

'I remember. Yes, see you there, but don't let Felipe give you a lift.'

'I'll come in my own car,' she promised.

'That jeep?'

Hannah smiled smugly. 'Carlos bought me a BMW—scarlet.'

Ramón's face was a picture. She almost felt sorry for him, so taken aback was he. 'A car? I must confess I thought Carlos was a figment of your imagination.'

She grinned. 'I know you did. You can come round and see it if you like. Esteban is bringing it from the garage after I get back. I might even let you drive it.'

'He must think a lot of you, Day,' he commented.

'Well, we aren't terribly close. I'd describe it as steady.'

'I see.' He studied her face, but she retained her innocent expression. Finally he said, 'Well, good luck to you. Go on getting better.' He went to the door. 'I'll bring a Sister next time.' Hannah looked after the closing door with yearning. With all his problems, Ramón could still joke with her a little. That was something that other people didn't see. She touched her buttock in the place he had slapped, and hid a smile. That was something not even her closest friends would hear about!

Her last visitor was Felipe Piedras. He came round the door tentatively, his handsome face serious, clutching a large bundle of red roses, deep and fragrant. She said before he could speak, 'It wasn't your fault, Felipe.'

He came straight to the bed. 'I was going too fast. I'll never forget the sight of you, the red blood on your pale cheek.' His voice was taut with feeling. 'You ought to sue me, you know. I was at fault.'

'Come off it, Felipe. I'm all right, aren't I? I even feel better for a couple of weeks' rest. No harm done.'

'There might have been.'

Suddenly she saw real tears in his eyes. She held out her arms, and he hugged her close for a long time. When he stood back, he wiped his eyes. 'It has just been a shock,' he muttered.

'It's been harder for you,' Hannah pointed out.

'The hospital kept it from the papers. But my wife will find out.'

'Not from me she won't.'

He shook his head, pacing up and down. '*Preciosa*, I was only just getting to know you.' He sat down at last. 'I'm getting a new car, from Leon. I saw your little BMW round at the back. Very nice.'

She nodded. 'Esteban will be relieved that I finally own a car fit for a doctor.'

He looked at her, his brown eyes full of meaning. 'You are sure you are all right?'

'Absolutely.'

'Then perhaps I will start sleeping at night.'

At five o'clock, Pablo Rodriguez came to take her back to their house. They were waiting at the main road for a gap in the traffic when Hannah turned back to gaze at the hospital. Pablo, plump and jolly, said, 'If you were looking for Ramón, he has already left.'

She straightened herself in her seat. 'Oh.'

'Hannah, I feel you ought not to be too fond of that man,' Pablo said earnestly.

'I'm not fond of him at all.' They drove along the highway for a while then Hannah said, 'When are you taking blood again, Pablo?'

'At the Villa Pandora. We are invited to the big dinner party Benito is giving. You will be there?'

'I will, yes.'

'Good. Then I can rely on you to prevent him from

disappearing into the undergrowth when I take out my syringe.'

'My pleasure.' Her imagination ran riot at the picture of Ramón crawling away into the bushes at the sight of the needle.

Pablo said, 'The last test was almost unchanged, but the liver function was very slightly improved. And he is certainly working harder with no side effects.'

'That's marvellous news!' smiled Hannah.

'Mmm.' He smiled too at her enthusiasm. 'You two were always prickly together. There was a violent reaction when your name came into the conversation. Similarly with you.'

'I'm grateful to him for the operation,' she assured him.

'It was a good one. We both know that glass can't be seen on X-ray—so you will report back if you have the slightest symptoms that might mean a piece has been left in?'

'I will, Pablo. And I'm not in love with him—he's only a friend, you know.' She crossed her fingers.

CHAPTER NINE

HANNAH woke up in Dolores' spare room. It was a small house, set in its own little garden, hedged by hibiscus and squat palm trees. She heard the couple breakfasting, and decided that she would only be an extra liability if she stayed on. When Dolores brought her a pretty tray, with scrambled eggs, toast and coffee, she explained how well she felt. 'I think I should get back home. Esteban is living in the hospital while I've been away. Would you be an angel and ask him to come and get me?'

Dolores had to agree. She could see that Hannah felt unsettled, and wanted to get back to her own familiar surroundings. 'I think I would feel the same. It hasn't been easy for you—there might have been a scandal. But Inés isn't like that—Felipe will explain. It's all over now.'

Hannah smiled, recognising the little lecture. 'No more lifts from married men for me, you mean? I'll do my best.' There was a hoot from the drive outside and Hannah looked out of the window, and laughed outright. 'And there's the very reason why I'll be fine from now on. My very own transport!' She waved to Esteban through the open shutters.

Dolores cried out in admiration. In the brilliance of the morning sun, the scarlet of the BMW was positively luminous. 'Now we will always be able to find you!'

They went to the door, and Dolores gave Hannah's bag to Esteban to put in the boot. Esteban said, 'She is so beautiful to drive.'

'Let me try,' said Hannah.

Pablo had come to the door on hearing the horn. 'No, Hannah, take it easy for two more weeks. Gentle exercise—short walks, and back to your swimming. But Esteban must drive you for two weeks.'

Hannah said goodbye to her friends. 'I can't begin to

thank you. I'll come and see you soon.' She got into the
passenger seat, fastened her belt. 'Will you say thank
you again to Ramón?'

Pablo nodded, and smiled his dimpled smile. 'I think
he knows you are grateful. And he is only thankful that
the injury was no worse.'

As Esteban eased out on to the main road, Dolores
called, 'And make sure Pepe brings you food every
night!'

'Does the doctor not allow me to cook for myself?'
called Hannah.

Pablo laughed. 'You cannot cook. You will starve.'

'I can learn. Why not?' She waved as they found a
space in the traffic, and Esteban put his foot down, a
blissful smile on his face.

He parked on the dusty verge at the front of the
hospital. Hannah said, 'Esteban, could you get a couple
of men to help you concrete this over? The dust may go
into the engine.'

He grinned broadly. 'Never before did you mind the
dust.'

Hannah gazed at the shiny paintwork of her lovely
car. 'I think I'm going to be very fussy, Esteban. Where
is the jeep?'

'Round the side.'

'Good. I won't want to take the BMW out on rough
roads.'

'But she is made for strong work too. And I promise I
will clean her every day.' They went up the hospital
path. Hannah reached for her key, while her chauffeur
stood back; the mistress was home, and he was no longer
in charge here. She went into the front porch, shadowy
because of the closed shutters against the heat of the sun.
A sweet smell filled the air, and as her eyes got used to
the dark, she saw that the hall was lined with red roses.

She turned to Esteban, shaking her head in exasper-
ation. 'Felipe certainly knows how to say he's sorry,' she
remarked.

'You like them? He sent them this morning. I think he
telephoned to Dr Rodriguez to ask when you would
come home.'

'It's a sweet idea, but I wish he wouldn't,' said Hannah. 'It embarrasses me.'

They went inside, and Esteban put her bag in her room. She went out to the verandah, past yet more vases filled with roses. Esteban followed her, and handed her an envelope. 'Señor Piedras asked to give you this also,' he said.

Hannah opened the envelope. Inside was a cheque —for the exact the amount she had paid for the car. She stared at it, uncomprehending for a moment. The boy said, 'He bought the car for you. He called it compensation.'

'But I can't possibly . . .' she began.

'He told me that if he had to pay in the courts, he would pay much more than ten thousand pesetas.'

'But I'm not taking him to court!'

Esteban shrugged, and Hannah realised it was something she must take up with Felipe himself. She sat down on her own chair, leaning her head back in the sun, listening to her beloved breakers, rolling and ebbing over the familiar grey sand. It was good to be home. The last few weeks had been dreamlike. But she was herself again, she was whole in body and mind—and almost cured of her passion for Ramón Riviero. He could stay in the past too. She would let the waves wash away the hurt that his name always caused in her heart. If possible . . .

There was a shout from the beach path and Hannah opened her eyes, to see Carla running up the steps. 'You are home! You feel OK now?'

'I'm fine, Carla. How are you? I must owe you a month's wages by now.'

'Never mind. You have had a very bad experience, Dr Hannah. Forget money until work starts again.'

'Work?' Hannah looked around her. 'I wonder . . . ?'

'You don't want to leave San Agustín?'

'No.' But her tone was hesitant.

Carla said, 'You sit here, out of the sun. I will bring you coffee, made the way you like it.'

But Hannah followed her into the kitchen. 'Carla, you're a good cook?' she asked.

'I like cooking,' Carla agreed.

'Do you think you could teach me a few basics? Rice, for a start? And roast lamb with peppers and garlic?'

The woman looked delighted. 'Sure. What do you like for lunch? We can start now, make a beautiful lunch for you and me and Esteban? Paella? Scampi? What would you like?'

'Chilli beans, Carla,' smiled Hannah. 'I haven't had that for ages.'

'That is one of the easy ones. Come, I will make a list. After coffee, I will buy from the shop for you.'

'Great! The nurse becomes the chef, and the doctor is to be the kitchenmaid. I like it!' They went off to the verandah to plan the day's menu.

They cooked rather more chilli beans than they needed, with much laughter and joking. Esteban kept getting in the way, until Hannah despatched him to find Rosita, and bring her to join the feast. Hannah was laughing at the mess she had made in the kitchen. 'Will I ever get the smell of garlic from my hands?' she wanted to know.

'Not if you go on cutting it up as though you were squeezing it first.'

Hannah looked around for a clear bit of space on the whitewood table, but her first attempts at cookery were not very tidy. 'There are too many small things, like salt, and spices, and ginger,' she said. 'I see my mind is very untidy yet. I'll need plenty of practice!'

'Never mind, the smell is good, Dr Hannah.' Carla had lifted the lid on the simmering concoction. 'I think you have passed your first test.'

And then there were footsteps and Esteban came running in, followed very closely by Rosita—and by the unmistakable figure of Ramón Riviero. 'Dr Riviero was with Señora Alfonso, so he said he would like to lunch with us also,' Rosita explained.

Hannah's breath seemed suddenly unsteady. She faced him, admiring his tall figure in slim jeans and a checked shirt. So he had been with Rosita. She said huskily, 'Now you all know that this is my first attempt?'

Rosita ran across and gave her a little hug. 'You look

well, Dr Hannah, but surely you should not be working so hard?'

'I call this occupational therapy.' The atmosphere, strained at first, now relaxed, and the jokes began about Hannah's talents.

Rosita said, 'I will bring some wine to go with this feast.' And she ran out, to return swiftly with an earthenware jug from her mother's house. They all sat round the wooden table, which Carla scrubbed to get rid of the smell of garlic, before covering it with a flowered tablecloth. They looked like a family, rather than business associates.

Hannah smiled, 'Now I know why I was in such a hurry to come home!'

Carla said, 'You wanted to test out your newest talent.' And in the middle of the laughter, she saw that Ramón was looking relaxed and almost happy too.

But after the meal, Rosita insisted that Hannah go and rest. And indeed, it had been a boisterous homecoming, and she was very tired. She left them all looking for aprons in order to wash the dishes. She thought the sound of their laughter would keep her awake, but she fell asleep almost at once.

She didn't know what woke her, then she saw the steaming cup beside her. One of her kind friends had brought her a cup of tea, and crept away when they saw she was still sleeping. She sat up. Yes, she was stiffer than she expected. Her back still ached. But she was home, where she wanted to be. She drank the hot tea, and felt better. She wondered who was still here. Probably Carla. Carla was middle-aged, and had no family, so the clinic had in a way become her family. Hannah got up, straightened her back, and found she felt better, rested and relaxed. She pulled on her blue dress and brushed her hair.

She took the cup to the kitchen—impeccably tidy. But no one was there. Siesta time, probably, although it was after four. Hannah wandered out to the verandah and saw someone sitting on her favourite chair. Ramón turned as he heard the swish of her bare feet over the mat. She said unsteadily, 'The others have all gone?'

'Yes.' He stood up, with unusual politeness, until she had sat opposite him. 'Where did the roses come from? Carlos?'

Hannah smiled and looked down nervously. 'Well, yes, the same man as the car.' She had started this fiction, so it was better to keep it up. And anyway, the roses and the car had been provided—accidentally—by the same man. 'He's generous.'

'A bit over the top, isn't it—all these flowers?' commented Ramón.

She said defensively, 'Flowers make a woman feel good sometimes.'

Ramón didn't answer, and she wondered why he had stayed. She looked across at him, suddenly feeling happy that he was there opposite to her as he used to be. The line from the song came into her head: 'I've grown accustomed to his face . . .'

Hannah said hesitantly, 'You have things to do in San Agustín?'

Frankly, Ramón said, 'It gets harder to go back. Benito is so smug. He thinks I have capitulated—that I will make no more protests about the way he treats the men.'

'So what's the next step?'

'Damned if I know. He does not dream that he could ever be in the wrong.'

Hannah looked down again, saying rather wickedly, 'I always wondered where you got it from.'

He waited until she looked up and met his dark gaze, then he nodded. 'I am very like him, I know—that's why it is so hard. We can't go on together. I have to beat him. And—Hannah, I don't know how.' And he put his face into his hand for a moment. She realised that there were few people with whom he was so open, allowing her to see his vulnerability, and she wished with all her heart that she could do something to help.

She said quietly, to make conversation, 'You like working at Santa Teresa's?'

'Not so much as here.'

'You could come back.'

'You cannot be starting work so soon,' he said firmly.

'You need a rest first.'

'I know. I wondered whether to go to England. I have some distant cousins. And my university friends . . .'

'You never talked about your home before.'

'Well, we were always arguing, weren't we?'

Ramón looked across at her, and sat up straighter in his chair. The sun was low in the sky, the sunbathers beginning to cover up their redness, especially the topless ones, beginning to look around for a cool drink. Pedro began to fold up the umbrellas. 'I know I used to be extremely rude,' Ramón admitted.

She smiled. 'It doesn't matter now.'

'Can I do anything for you before I go? I could drive you to Mogan to see your Carlos. It is on my way, and you look rather small and lonely.'

Hannah shook her head. 'A woman alone is a—what did you say—a sorry sight?'

He met her teasing with a natural smile. 'It did take me a long time to get over the shock of being sent to ask a woman for a job. I must remember to have words with Pablo about that. It was a dirty trick.'

She felt a wave of sympathy for him. 'You were very depressed, Ramón. And it was made worse by not even being able to get drunk to ease the pain now and then.'

'You don't have to make excuses for me.' He didn't mention his illness, but he didn't mind her referring to it. He said suddenly, 'You don't look comfortable. Wait.' He got to his feet and went inside, coming out immediately with a cushion. 'Here.' His hands were gentle as he positioned the cushion behind her back, his breath warm on her cheek.

'You've already done enough by operating. You don't have to nurse me as well,' Hannah protested.

He stood for a moment looking down at her. She wanted to beg him to stay, but her pride prevented her. Ramón said, 'Well, apart from strangling Felipe, I can't think of anything else I can do to help you.'

'Thank you.' Her words were almost a whisper. It was agony to have to say goodbye.

He nodded briefly. 'See you, Day.' He stood back, as though afraid to come any nearer, then he turned and ran down the steps.

The sound of his footsteps faded. Her heart went with him. What a difference today from that brutal chauvinist who had walked into her life along that very path! Hannah sat until the shadows from the palm trees reached her feet, the children had gone from the beach, and the first star was out. Then she gave a huge sigh, turned and locked the door, and went down the steps to the beach path, along it to Pepe's. 'A large gin and tonic, Pepe,' she said.

His face brightened. 'Hey, doctor, you are better, huh?' He gave her the tallest gin she had ever had. 'On me. Welcome home.'

Hannah sat on her usual stool, listening to the murmur of conversation, the chink of glasses, the laughter from groups of friends. And then the guitar began. She said, 'He's good, Pepe.'

'He plays well. Brandy money.'

The thrilling ripple of notes cascaded round them, and Hannah listened, almost in tears. Then she put two thousand-peseta notes into an envelope and handed it to Pepe. 'Give him that.' The music trembled, sobbed, pierced into her very soul.

Hannah's life for the next two weeks continued in the same casual holiday manner. She joined the idle tourists, sunbathed, learned more about cooking. By the end of that time her tan was perfected, her scar almost disappeared. She felt strong and content. She would start driving her car next week, and then she would open the hospital for business as usual.

And then, by post this time, came the invitation to dinner with Benito Riviero again. She looked at the elaborate lettering, the gilded edges. She didn't think of the hit she had been last time; she didn't even worry too much about what to wear. As she fingered the small card, all she knew was that she hadn't seen Ramón for two weeks, and that she missed him terribly. And her heart quickened, because she would see him again soon.

The telephone rang. It was morning, and Hannah was

still alone in the hospital. She went through to answer it.
'Hello?'

'Hannah, my *preciosa*! What a joy to hear your voice!'

'Hello, Felipe. Thank you for the roses, but please
don't send any more. I'm better now.' He had sent roses
twice more since that first extravagant gesture.

'Allow me to ease my own conscience,' said Felipe.
'You have received an invitation from the Villa
Pandora?'

'Yes. Have you?'

'I have. And I offer you my car and my protection as
your escort—to show you have forgiven me, and that
you trust me again to drive you.'

'That would be terribly unwise, and you know it,'
Hannah told him firmly.

'Fair enough. I thought I would try my luck.'

'I'll be driving myself,' she told him.

'Then will you come out for a boat trip with me?'

'Felipe, you are incorrigible!' she laughed.

'No, darling—a romantic.'

'At least we understand one another.' She enjoyed his
whimsical and worldly attitude. 'I'll see you at Benito's.'

'But how can I survive until then? Allow me a little
into your life. Hannah, you know as well as I do that we
only have each other.'

'That's a terrible lie and you know it.'

'You know how to hurt a man!' he grimaced.

'And you know how to seduce a woman while your
wife is away. Well, try someone less gullible.'

'Hannah Day, I almost killed you. Let me see you just
for that.' And there was a raw need in his voice that just
might have been genuine.

'Felipe, I'd like to stay friends,' Hannah said gently.

'Then allow me to call and see you one day soon.'

'All right.' She would do no harm by chatting to him.

'You treat yourself well!'

'And you're very big headed,' she retorted.

After the conversation, Hannah wondered if she had
done the right thing. He was a married man, and
Dolores had warned her about getting her name linked
with his. In a way, Felipe was right—she didn't have

anyone else. She was lonely, and she enjoyed his company. It was tempting. One small affair could harm no one. Yet a still small voice somewhere kept telling her to be careful.

She was looking out at the beach next day. There was a group of particularly plump ladies, their stomachs poking out from tight bathing costumes, their husbands wearing 'I love Canaria' hats, and eating large ice-creams. And her thoughts turned suddenly to what Ramón had told her about India. The idea began to buzz round in her head. Why not leave for an extended tour of duty in the Third World? There was so much need at the moment. She could rent out the hospital—Dr Arora would be interested, she knew—and apply for a two-year stint in India. The fat ladies let out a coarse screech of laughter. Hannah went in, and wrote out an enquiry to the World Health Organisation. It would do no harm to show interest. And it might also be the best treatment for her own shattered heart.

She would miss San Agustín; it was home to her now. But by writing a letter, she was not committing herself. She put the folded letter in an airmail envelope. No stamp. She put the letter on the hall table, to remind her to buy some stamps when she went out.

The footsteps on the verandah were light, and at first she couldn't identify them. She went out, only to collide with the tall lithe figure of Felipe, erect and smilingly confident in white trousers and a fawn shirt, his greying hair attractively waving round his ears, his keen amused eyes gazing at her with admiration. It was a hard package to resist—almost aggressively male, yet warm and affectionate. And he made her laugh. Hannah needed to laugh more. She didn't want a lover, but she yearned to be happy.

Felipe said nothing at first, merely caught her by the hands to steady her, and stood back to look down into her face. 'So, my dear, you will not drive to Benito's with me?'

She smiled. 'I shall go in my own BMW. And incidentally, you forgot something.' And she took her hands away from his to bring the envelope with his cheque in. 'I want to buy my own car, Felipe.'

His face changed. 'Hannah, please. I owe you—so much. If you refuse this miserly sum, then I shall insist you go to litigation, and you will be awarded very much more.'

'I don't want to argue. But my injuries are completely healed. You owe me nothing.'

She had never seen Felipe so serious. He pleaded with her. 'I could not rest. I acted so foolishly. I will never forget it—ever. The sound of the car crunching as it turned over on those rocks . . . the screech as the metal tore the metal of the crash barrier.'

They argued for a long time. Finally Hannah agreed to take half the price of the car. 'Now, can we just be friends again? she asked.

'That I like very much. The boat trip?'

'No. You have a wife, man!'

'So, no boat trip, and no company for me to Benito's.' Felipe feigned sadness. 'Now I am the one with the sorrowful countenance.'

'I'll look out for you at Benito's,' promised Hannah. 'There's a shortage of intelligent men. But I'll drive myself there and back.'

'Ah, Hannah—you treat me badly now!'

'Find someone willing. You're too masculine for me.'

'No, no. I know what it is—I am just not the right one for you.'

'Felipe, don't psycho-analyse me!' Hannah said crossly.

He smiled, his white, charming crooked smile. 'I wouldn't dream of it.' And before she knew what was happening, he had caught her to him and kissed her lips with his gentle, persuasive technique that he knew she had been unable to resist last time.

She disengaged herself gently. 'Goodbye, Felipe.'

He made no fuss. 'Good night, my *preciosa*.' And as he walked jauntily along the passage, he picked up her letter. 'You want me to post this?'

'It needs a stamp—airmail.'

'I'll take it for you. Why are you writing to WHO?'

'I thought I might go to India,' she told him.

His face went blank. 'India? Oh no, Hannah, not another ministering angel!'

'It's my business. I'm not forcing you to post it for me.'

'I'll take it. But are you sure Ramón hasn't been putting ideas into your head?'

'At first, I suppose. But I feel I could be of use, while I'm still young and strong.'

'There are poor people in Canaria,' Felipe pointed out.

'Yes. But it isn't quite the same as having no doctor and no hope of a hospital, is it?'

'I'll post your letter, my sweet. May I see you again?'

'I'm sure we'll run into one another.'

Hannah went inside, and started to peel an onion, a pepper and a tomato to fry together before making an omelette. Carla's lessons had been successful, and her pupil was now almost self-sufficient in the kitchen. She thought of Felipe as she worked. So very nice a man —too charming to be left alone so much. Surely his wife would be happier with such a husband than going off with her mother? Unless she too had other affairs. Felipe did say she did exactly what she pleased . . .

She heard footsteps. Carla, probably; only hospital staff walked in without knocking. She stirred the onion, and turned the heat down while she turned to look for paprika and black pepper. Felipe Piedras was back, in his hands two triangular glasses. 'I thought we could have a dry Martini before lunch,' he announced.

Hannah giggled, 'Talk about cheek!'

He sat down without being asked, and handed her a glass. They sat at opposite sides of the table, sipping the drinks. Then Felipe said, 'I have realised that no one can compete with Ramón for your attention. When you are in a room together, even though you do not touch, you seem to exclude the rest of the world. I would be the happiest man in the world to have a woman so deep in love as that with me—to make love without even touching. That man does not know what a treasure is there for the taking.'

'You know more than I do. Are you sure of your diagnosis?' She tried to make light of his words, though they touched her heart where it hurt.

'I am a romantic, my angel. I study women as others study economics.'

'Felipe, I cannot understand why your wife is not blissfully happy with you,' Hannah sighed.

'Simple—she isn't a romantic. Her mother selected me as a suitable match. I think I married her mother as well—she is always around! They meet to spend money on clothes and diamonds. My pearls of words fall on deaf ears, because they do not sparkle like diamonds.'

'But roses—did you never send her roses?'

'She can buy her own.' He sat for a while, gazing out at the ever-changing sea, at the crowded beach and the sparkling water beyond. 'Why not come to me, *querida*, and let the sound of the waves sweep over us, drown out the weariness of real life?' he looked across the table, but made no attempt to move. 'Why won't you come to me? Who else have either of us got today, my Hannah?'

'You're too clever. You know I can't come, however beautiful are your words—or your roses.'

'Who do we harm?'

She didn't answer, because she knew an affair with Felipe would harm no one. He went on talking, his voice quite enchanting in its tone and the gentleness, the pathos of his arguments. 'I wish we had met long ago, Hannah. Funny how some people manage to creep into your heart—exchange a few words of affection, laugh together at the same things . . . an episode, a passing dream in the moonlight . . .'

Then he seemed to give up. Draining his glass, he stood up. Hannah also stood to turn off the gas under her pan. In a moment, Felipe had caught her in his embrace, not trying to kiss her, but just holding her close, with both arms, in a gesture of affection and trust. 'Right action, wrong man?' he whispered.

'You're making it up about me and Ramón, you know,' said Hannah.

He let her go, shrugging his shoulders as he turned away. 'What are we going to do to help that man against his father, Hannah? He cannot do it alone.'

She was greatly relieved that the subject of romance

had been changed. She said eagerly, 'I was thinking, Felipe—when we're all there at the dinner table, you and I could start a conversation. I could ask innocently what is this I hear about unrest among the men. You would explain that they want more money. And then he would have to explain why he won't give it. Do you think we could steer the conversation?'

'We will try. I am tired of hearing tales of hardship from the men's leaders. Yes, go ahead. I will try to sit opposite to you, so that they can all hear what we say.'

'Well done, Felipe! I thought you wouldn't have the guts.'

'I suppose I have more to lose than you. But I'm willing to try.'

'Thank you, Felipe. Do you think you ought to warn Ramón what we plan?'

'I might. But it may be better to be spontaneous, otherwise he would get very nervous, and look even more lugubrious than usual.'

Hannah was quick to defend Ramón. 'He isn't lugubrious with me.' She stood for a minute, suddenly sad. 'Last time he was here—he has never been so pleasant. Explaining why he used to be ill-mannered . . . almost as if he wanted to make peace with me, before saying goodbye . . .' She turned away. Why hadn't she realised at the time? He had been making sure things were right between them, making sure that her imaginary friend in Mogan—her very own Carlos—was around to care for her. It was all so plain now: 'Ramón was planning not to see her again. She said very dully, 'He was saying goodbye.'

Felipe watched her for a moment. She didn't want to tell him to leave, but she very much wanted to be alone just then. He said softly, 'Hannah, Hannah, why don't we forget everything that hurts, and run away together?'

She smiled. 'Felipe, why don't you try your remarkable powers of manipulation on your own wife?'

'Because she only listens to her mother.'

'Then I prescribe a quick course in manipulating the mother.'

'My angel, she is as ugly as the back of a camel!' he laughed.

'It just might be worth it. Use your talents where they'll make you happy. Try it.'

He went to the door, and Hannah walked with him. At the door he turned. 'Good luck, angel.'

'And you, Felipe.

'Maybe in twenty years all will be well.' He leaned over and kissed the top of her head. 'Pity about now, though, isn't it?'

'Señora Piedras might not agree!' Hannah said drily.

'Good luck in the Third World.'

'God bless you, Felipe. She watched him stroll down to his new pale green Mercedes and drive away without looking back.

CHAPTER TEN

ON THE DAY of Benito Riviero's dinner party, Hannah was already keyed up when she awoke. Today was the day she was going to do something genuine to help Ramón. She wasn't exactly sure what, but the adrenalin started pumping as she got out of bed. When she looked at her limp hair in the mirror, she marched straight out and took herself to the best hairdresser in Las Palmas. 'Yes, *señorita*. You would like a cut? Very wise. The *señorita*'s hair holds a natural wave. The length prevents the curl. A cut would bring out the full beauty. And the colour—it is ravishing!'

Back at the hospital, she wasn't quite sure what she had done. It did look good round her slim face and grey eyes, the hair lifted like a halo.. She shook it vigorously. It still looked exquisite. She ran her fingers through it several times. It still looked good.

Somehow, the evening loomed very large in her mind. She had already applied to work in the Third World. This might be the very last capitalist function she attended. From now on she could look forward to seeing the very lives that Ramón had told her about, stories she had listened to so attentively, but never thought she herself would be called. After her bath, she wandered out on to the verandah to watch her favourite evening sunshine. She had only been standing a few minutes, wearing only a thin summer dress, when a man came running up to her as though he were competing in some beach Olympics. '*Medico?*' he gasped.

'*Si, medico.*'

'*Mi mujer—por favor, vengo conmigo!*'

Hannah forgot she was on holiday, that the hospital would be closing for the betterment of the Third World. She ran indoors and grabbed her white coat and her emergency bag. 'OK—*vamos!*' she said hurriedly.

They were on the beach before Hannah remembered

that she was closed. No matter—someone needed her.
The man's wife was lying on the sand, her pretty going-
out dress rumpled and grey with the sand. The couple
had obviously been beginning a night out. Hannah knelt
beside her, taking her wrist to feel the pulse while taking
a careful look at her face, eyes and expression. 'What is
the trouble, *señora*?' she asked gently.

'My legs—they will not hold me.'

Hannah examined in silence. Heart and lungs were
OK. Abdomen, fundi had no abnormality. The central
nervous system—might she have had a stroke? Hannah
was meticulous in her examination, but there were no
abnormal reflexes at all. Then perhaps the lady was
faking. And if so, why so? She said gently, 'Will you try
to stand if I hold you?'

'I will try.'

'Let's give it a go, then.'

The husband tried to speak, and Hannah noticed that
the wife interrupted at once. 'Go away! Let me talk to
the doctor.'

Hannah's suspicious antennae began to suspect something psychological. She said in the lady's ear, 'Your
husband was very worried about you.'

The woman looked almost pleased. 'The fool! He
does not care.'

Hannah was even more confirmed in her diagnosis. 'I
can't believe that. He sounded so worried when he came
to call me.'

'But he was not even here! We were to meet at Pepe's,
but he did not come for so long. He said it was business,
but I know where he was. He spends all the time he has
in the café where the women wear no clothes.' There
were tears in her eyes, and Hannah sympathised. This
was almost a violation of his marriage vows. Hannah
helped her very slowly to her feet. The woman tottered,
but did not fall. Hannah turned to the husband, who was
hovering.

'Please—leave her with me for a while. I'll examine
her in my hospital. Please come back in one hour.'

Arm in arm, the two women walked very slowly to the
hospital. Hannah's anxiety to get to San Nicolás was

pushed to the back of her mind. There was no problem with the patient's walking mechanism; it was all in the mind. And from what she had said already, she felt very alone and unwanted. Hannah knew what it felt like. She took her to the consulting room, sat her down, and made them both a cup of tea. No doubt at the Villa Pandora they were consuming champagne. But this lady was a gentle soul, totally unused to explaining to her husband how alone she felt.

'You must tell him,' Hannah said firmly.

'He is a man, doctor. He does not want to know.'

Hannah smiled. 'You want me to give you some lessons?'

The woman made an attempt at a chuckle. 'You can teach me? These men, they are all so selfish.'

Hannah thought of Felipe Piedras. Was he selfish, or merely neglected by his wife? She said, 'Maybe. But it's not necessarily a permanent condition.'

'I have never met such a kind doctor before,' the woman said fervently.

'You've tried this before? My dear, it won't work—he won't understand. I'll have a word with him—make it clear that every action of his matters to you.'

The woman looked up at Hannah with wide, worried brown eyes. 'Do you think he will listen?'

'I think so. Now, finish your tea. I'll go and meet the enemy.'

The husband was waiting outside, afraid to knock on the door. Hannah went out to him, closing the door behind her. She was already late for her dinner. She took the man to the verandah. In her best Spanish, she explained, 'What a lucky man you are!—to have a woman so devoted to you that she reacts to every move you make. Now, do you think you deserve such devotion?' She did her best, and by the end of her talk, the man was almost weeping.

'I will care for her, I will,' he said fervently. 'She is a treasure.'

Hannah watched them go, the man holding his wife round the waist with tenderness. It would not last, perhaps. On the other hand, her words might have helped to save a marriage. Hannah had not wasted her time. She went indoors, locking the door. In her room, she brought out her black dress—sleek and backless, with gold jewellery. It showed off her figure. Very slowly the feeling of power, of euphoria, came back. She quickly applied blusher, lipstick, perfume, and brushed her hair back, holding it with a single gold pin. It fluffed round her head now. She smiled back at her reflection. This might be the very last capitalist dinner she would have on Canaria. May it be a success.

She drove with a frisson of excitement to San Nicolás. She had not driven so far in her new scarlet car, but it handled perfectly. She twisted and turned along the mountain trail after Mogan, the headlights showing her the dangers in good time. She saw the walls of the Villa Pandora, floodlit. And the gate—already open, with a guard at each side. And in the middle of the path . . . She braked quickly.

'I have been ringing San Agustín. I thought perhaps you had forgotten.'

Hannah's heart leapt. It was Ramón, casual in his red silk shirt and dark trousers. The engine still running, she got out of the car, as Ramón snapped his fingers and a footman ran to park it for her. She walked up the fragrant drive with him, the peacocks making their loud croaking calls.

Before they reached the front door Ramón stopped. Almost against his will, he said, 'You look lovely, Hannah.' He reached out and plucked a milky white orchid from the hedge. 'Here. You told me women like flowers.'

She found a small pin in her handbag. She pinned it to her dress, her heart pounding. 'Thank you, Riviero. That was thoughtful.'

'You are very late,' he remarked. 'Did you do it on purpose? Did you think it would intrigue me?'

'I never gave you a thought. I had an interesting case of hysterical paralysis. It took me a while to sort it out.' But she exulted that he was worried—that he had actually come to the gates to look for her. She tried not to look into his darkly beautiful face. 'Shall we go?' she said. 'I must apologise to your father.'

They walked in together. The front door was wide open, and Rosita's uncle stood deferentially. Hannah stopped and said, 'Good evening. You are well?'

'Very well, *señorita*.' The man looked surprised that a guest had troubled to speak to him. But Hannah saw that Ramón looked pleased. He was thrillingly handsome in the red silk shirt. His face was more haggard, though, his eyes suspiciously bright. She worried about him. Pablo was to take a blood sample tonight. Please God there would be some improvement this time!

Hannah said to Ramón, 'Your father keeps well?'

'Never changes. A little short of breath.'

'He should take more exercise. Take him riding with you.'

Then Benito came out of the lounge, in his well-cut suit, alerted by the butler, Gabrielo. 'Hannah, I was worried about you! My evening was not complete until you came.' He bent over her hand. 'Come and join the company. I think you know everybody.' Hannah entered the lounge in front of Benito, and there was an audible gasp of appreciation from the Latin men, a haughty gaze of interest from the women.

Pablo and Dolores were almost the last to greet her, as champagne was handed liberally round. Dolores said, 'You are going to be in demand tonight—you look wonderful! So I will tell you now that Pablo has taken Ramón's blood sample, and the messenger is on his way to Las Palmas laboratory.'

'And are you hopeful?' asked Hannah.

Pablo smiled. 'Yes, Hannah. Hopeful—and devout.'

'I'll pray too,' Hannah promised.

Dolores was wearing dark green ruffles, and her dark hair rippled down her back. She said, 'I think you will be surrounded by men tonight, Hannah. If I don't see you again, I'll phone you with Ramón's results.'

'Thank you.' Hannah felt she had to tell her best friend what she had done. 'Dolores, I want you to know—I've applied to go and work in India.'

'Oh no—you can't!' Dolores exclaimed. 'It is Ramón —he put you up to it.' She was distressed.

'He first made me think. But the decision is mine,' Hannah told her firmly.

Then Dolores was elbowed out by the man who had bored Hannah last time. A glass of champagne was put in her hand. As last time, the men were too tall for Hannah to see where Ramón had got to, but Felipe made good use of experienced elbows, and put himself at her side. 'You are magnificent tonight, angel.' His tiger-brown eyes looked down into hers, against considerable opposition from three other men. He looked daggers at someone who had dared to put a hand on her bare back. 'The lady is just recovering from a serious injury.'

'Caused by you, I hear?'

But Felipe was not to be abashed. 'She was with me at the time.' He sounded quite proud.

Dinner was served. As Felipe escorted Hannah, she whispered, 'I hope you haven't lost your nerve.'

He grinned. 'I'm a gambler, angel. Take it away, and *suerte!*'

The meal was lavish and superbly cooked, from the oysters and lobster to the soup, then a sorbet, followed by suckling pig. The white linen shone, the crystal and silver gleamed. Hannah ate little, her feelings over-excited by what she had to do that night.

The bombe surprise was followed by cheese and fresh fruits. Hannah began to watch Benito, to listen to his conversation with the widow Lorenzo—again at his right hand, but with Ramón on her other side. She tried not to care. When compliments began to fall on the excellence of his dinner, Hannah suddenly gained enough confidence to lean across and say loudly, 'I'm proud to say I have met your father, Señor Riviero. It's a healthy life, up there in the mountains.'

It was obvious she had annoyed him by referring to his humble origins, but she was cheered by the sudden smile in Ramón's eyes as he looked across at her. 'Oh yes?' Benito didn't want to talk about it.

But Hannah hadn't finished yet. 'It must help you a lot in employing labour, to have worked on the land yourself.'

'Naturally, I treat them well.' Benito's lips pressed tightly together, and he looked around for another topic of conversation.

Hannah asked innocently, 'You must tell me what you think is a fair wage. I have two nurses, a maid and a chauffeur, and I do hope I'm not overpaying them.' She saw Ramón hide a sudden grin behind his napkin.

And then Ramón took up the fight. 'My father's doctrine is to pay as little as possible. Surely you know that is good business, Dr Day?'

Hannah spoke quickly, as she saw Benito preparing for a quick put-down. 'But surely, Dr Riviero, it's bad policy to have a resentful workforce? I depend on my staff's goodwill. It's a matter of life and death, you see.'

Ramón's answer was slick and almost could have been rehearsed. 'I agree. It is all a question of mutual support and dependency.'

Hannah saw Felipe studiously looking down. She said in a clear voice, now having the attention of the entire table, 'You must have a legal opinion on this, Señor Piedras?'

Felipe, to his eternal credit, did not try to get out of the question. 'My lovely *medico*, you speak sublime truth, as always. I think resentful workmen are dangerous workmen.'

Ramón stood up. 'As all our directors are here, I think it a good idea to put forward a motion that our men be given an immediate hundred per cent rise, to bring them back in line with inflation.'

The mutters and background chat were now almost deafening. Ramón sat down, and Benito stood up. At once the room became hushed. Benito stared angrily at his son. 'This is my company! Business matters will not be discussed at the dinner table!' His face had gone purple.

Ramón stood up opposite, glaring into his father's face. 'You are aware that some people have no dinner table, thanks to you?'

There was uproar. Hannah could see some people openly agreeing with Ramón. Benito shouted, 'Look at my Communist son, trying to ruin all my work! This is not a political meeting, Ramón. Go and get your Communist friends first, and try to make a revolution in San Nicolás! You will never succeed!'

And then there was a horrified silence, as Benito, almost in slow motion, doubled up, his face livid, a grimace on his lips, and slid groaning to the floor. Pablo was first at his side, and stood by him, shielding him. 'Clear the room,' he ordered. 'Please go outside while we give our host some air.'

The guests shuffled out. Pablo was muttering, 'There's no pulse!'

Hannah said, 'Keep thumping his chest. I've got my bag in the car.' She ran to get it, while Pablo gave cardiac massage. Ramón breathed lungfuls of air into Benito's mouth. Hannah called on her way back, 'I've got some atropine,' and Ramón stood back while she injected. She looked up at Ramón's sweaty, tragic face. 'If this doesn't work, can I try adrenalin?'

He nodded. 'Try everything.' He breathed again, while Pablo pressed and squeezed the fat body. Hannah filled the syringe with adrenalin. 'Show me the fourth intercostal space.' Ramón had his finger on the spot before she was ready. Hannah pushed the needle through the chest wall to the heart muscle. For a second, the body jerked, then Benito slumped. Ramón stopped respiration and Pablo stopped massage. With tears pouring down his cheeks, Ramón said, 'Our problems seem to be over.' He reached out a hand and closed his father's eyelids over staring eyes. Then he bent and laid his cheek against Benito's, sobbing quietly.

Pablo said, putting a hand on Ramón's shoulder, 'You want me to tell them?'

Ramón took a deep breath, and controlled his weeping. 'I'll do it. The whole thing is mine now.' They watched him straighten his back, wipe his eyes with the back of his hand before going to the door. They watched him, pitying his distress. The *padre* had been called, and he came hurrying into the room as Ramón left it. He knelt and intoned prayers in a low voice. Pablo said quietly, 'Their differences are settled.'

The guests began to leave, shuffling past the remote

figure of Ramón, who shook hands with each one as they passed him. He spoke in a low voice. 'There will be a meeting straight after the funeral. Yes, I was sincere about the wages. You can arrange it. Yes, I shall be in charge.' His face was set, the eyes large, dark and desperately sad. At last the stream of guests ended. Felipe, Hannah, Dolores and Pablo were the only ones to stay on. They sat in stunned silence until Ramón came back into the drawing room. The undertaker came out of the study with Gabrielo the butler. The body was now in respectful repose. Gabrielo saw the undertaker out, and came back with a tray of coffee and brandy.

Ramón came in, almost gaunt with weariness and shock, and Felipe went up to him. 'You want us to stay?'

Ramón looked round at them, but he couldn't speak. He sat down with them and covered his face with both hands. After a while he said, 'I had to do it. But I ought to have known what would happen. He always hated it when anyone told him he was in the wrong.'

Hannah had said nothing since Benito had died. Now she said in a low voice, 'I did it, Ramón. Don't you see? I came—planning it, meaning to do it. I didn't know how weak his heart must have been.'

She waited until Ramón turned towards her and faced her, his eyes again filling. He said, 'What you said was nothing to him. He would never have minded an argument with you. You did nothing. It was when I joined in that he resented it. Did you see his face? I can never forget it.' And it was Felipe who took a glass of brandy from the tray and put it into Ramón's hands. He drank it automatically, as a child would take a medicine from someone he trusted.

Hannah's voice was almost a whisper. 'People will say it was me.' She pressed her lips together, trying not to cry. The sense of guilt was overwhelming.

Ramón said loudly, 'No! If anyone is to blame it is he himself. He deserved it—that is what people will say.' He bent his head again with a grimace of anguish. 'Only he was my father. He did love me once—he always loved me when I didn't cross him——'

Hannah stood up and went out of the room, moving

like an automaton. She bent to collect her syringe, the empty ampoules of adrenalin and atropine, and put them in her black bag. Useless, they had been. A man had died. Hated or not, Benito had collapsed after she had challenged him. And in view of many people, too.

She stood up. She must go; there was nothing for her here. She walked to the door, but Ramón was standing there, blocking her way. She said, 'I'm sorry—I'm so sorry . . .'

'Stay for a while,' he said quietly.

'I can't. Everyone will know if I stay. They'll think we conspired to do it. I have to go away.'

'But I want you to stay.'

'I can't! Don't you see?' The others had come into the hall now. Pablo and Dolores were on their way down the steps. Gabrielo was standing on the steps, the only one there who showed no emotion. There was a gleam of triumph in his eyes. Hannah saw that few of Benito's staff would mourn for him. She looked back at Ramón. 'Goodbye. God bless you.' And she went down the steps. Her car was waiting in the drive. In the distance the flamingoes on the silver lake looked like a beautiful backdrop to their scene of tragedy. A peacock screeched in the garden, and was answered by another.

Hannah reached the car, but Ramón suddenly shouted, ran after her, and caught at her arm, twisting her round towards him. 'You are running out on me, Day!' His face was glazed, angry with her for what he saw as disloyalty.

She faced him, looked up into his distorted face. Words burst from her in time with sobs. 'Stop torturing me! Stop it—stop it!' And her voice faded into weary tears, her own mouth twisted with open crying.

Ramón seemed to remember himself, and a look of great yearning came over him. He opened his arms and caught her to him, and she gripped him equally strongly, straining him towards her, as though they wanted to shut out the rest of the world. She heard his sobs coming from deep in his chest.

It was Felipe who came to them, gently unwound their arms from each other. When Hannah looked up, there

were only the three of them left in the tranquil garden.
Ramón said, 'Take her home, then.' His voice was low
and resigned.

But Felipe's arm was on Ramón's shoulder; he had
recognised who needed him. 'She'll be all right.' To
Hannah he just nodded. 'I'll stay with him.' She nodded
back, filled with respect for Felipe's strength and loyalty.
She got in the car, but didn't start the engine until she
had seen both men go up the steps into the villa. She
heard scraps of what Felipe was saying. 'It's late. We
must let the servants go home.' By his gentle common
sense, he was gradually bringing Ramón back to reality,
to normality, and the realisation that things had to go on,
that someone must take over.

She hardly remembered the drive back down the dark
valley studded with the lights of San Nicolás, and then of
Mogan. She drove almost automatically. There was no
traffic about. She looked at her watch as she drew up on
the patch of scrub outside the hospital at San Agustín. It
was four in the morning.

Then she saw another car also parked off the road. It
was the Rodriguez' little Fiat, their second car. Dolores
got out when they saw Hannah's headlights, and went
across to the open car window. 'Hannah, leave the car
and come home with us.' Her gentle eyes were concerned. It was no use now saying that Ramón meant
nothing to her. They had seen it with their own eyes, and
they wanted to help.

Hannah said quietly, 'I want to stay by myself for a
long time, Dolores. I can't bear to talk. I want to
sleep—sleep for a long time.'

The other woman looked wise. 'That could be the best
way to get over it. But Hannah, it wasn't your fault
—please remember that.'

Hannah looked up into her friend's concerned face.
'Thank you. But it's been a bit of an earthquake for me.
Let me ring you in a couple of days.'

She watched them drive away, so content and happy
together, so kind and concerned for others. Dolores had
fallen for a steady reliable man; she couldn't possibly
understand what it was to be overwhelmed by a fiery

genius of a man who seemed sure he could never be happy on this earth. Yet perhaps she had seen a little of it tonight . . .

Hannah went to bed, throwing all her clothes and jewels on the floor. When she woke properly, it was four days later. She had got up and wandered about, drank a little water, eaten a biscuit or two, and gone straight back.

Four days—she sat up, and felt suddenly stronger, able to think straight again. She dressed in a simple skirt and peasant blouse, brushed back her shorn locks, and put the kettle on to make a large mug of tea. The sun poured in as always, the waves crashed on the shore, and the happy shouts of children filled the air. It was good to be alive. Yet the past events haunted her. She straightened up, finished her tea, and went to take the 'Closed' notice down from the front door. Work was the only thing. She must do what she was trained to do. Sitting around helped no one.

She looked through the circulars that had piled up behind the door. There was no answer yet from the World Health people. Hannah went to sit on the verandah, leaning back in pleasure at the warmth of the sun.

'Dr Hannah, are we open?' It was Rosita. 'Do you want some milk from Pepe?'

'Please. I drank my tea without.'

The girl was soon back, with fresh croissants and milk. 'Dr Hannah, I'm so proud of you,' she said earnestly. 'You are a heroine. There is no end to the praise.'

'A heroine? For being insolent to my host?'

The girl laughed, her eyes shining with happiness. 'I wanted to tell you yesterday, but you were asleep. You were brave enough to face him when no one else would.'

'Is that what the tale is?' Hannah began to feel more comfortable.

'Yes. And Ramón has given jobs back to every single man who was sacked. The wages are to be up at the end of the week. And he is re-organising the factory shifts, so that no one has to stay in the dust too long. It is so wonderful! Everyone is so happy.'

Hannah breathed a deep sigh. So all was now well.

Benito's death had brought about the benefits that had been sorely needed. It had been a painful and traumatic transition—but it was now complete. She picked up the phone. 'Dolores?' she said.

'Hannah—you are well?'

'Fine.'

'Then come to dinner.'

'I'll come at the weekend. I'm back to work now, and there's some catching up to do.'

Carla saw the open doors and came to join them next day. Both nurses told Hannah more of the local news. 'All the directors had talked with Ramón beforehand, so he knew he had their backing for the changes,' Carla told her. 'He is a happy man now—the gates of the Villa are left open. He goes riding each morning with the widow Lorenzo. Then he visits the plantations, and in the afternoons the factory. He is no longer working at the Las Palmas hospital. I suppose there is still much to see to.'

Hannah said, 'His name is cleared—that was all that mattered.' She knew Ramón would not come back to San Agustín. He had said his farewells, made his peace with her that last time on the verandah. The emotional night of the death, what either of them did and said, must be discounted as done in the heat of the moment. No, Ramón Riviero would not come back to San Agustín . . . It was sad, but inevitable. As Dolores said, Latin men are frequently attracted to others, but when they want to marry, they turn to their own. The widow Juana Lorenzo was rich, attractive, had a beautiful figure and, as far as Hannah knew, a nice enough nature.

Hannah went to the Rodriguez' home that following weekend. Benito had been dead for two weeks. There was no grieving for him in Pablo's house. 'Apart from obstinacy, Ramón had nothing in common with his father,' Pablo remarked.

'Arrogance?' suggested Hannah, with a smile. She wanted to convince them that the passionate embrace that night had meant nothing to her.

In the kitchen with Dolores, she said, 'I did love him once.'

'Not now?'

'No. He's in the past for me. I'm happy for him.'

'We are also happy,' said Dolores. 'It is a pity he had to leave his surgical work, but understandable, while he sorts things out. He is a man of considerable property now.'

The bell rang. It was Felipe Piedras. Hannah said, 'I didn't know you were invited.' She smiled as he came in, trying to control her impulse to ask more about Ramón. She must keep up the pretence before these three people. These were the only witnesses, and she had to act convincingly. They had to see that her love for Ramón was only that of a friend.

After the dinner, Felipe and Hannah walked in the garden, while Pablo went to help his wife make the coffee. It was Felipe who brought the subject up. 'So you are over this thing with Ramón?'

'He is part of my past, I assure you,' said Hannah.

'Good.' He put an arm around her waist. 'Because I am very lonely tonight.'

She recognised his advance—again the smooth, practised approach. She said pleasantly enough, 'It's sometimes very satisfying to be alone.'

He took his arm away. 'It's still there.'

'What is?'

'The wall—you and Riviero. There's no change.'

'I thought I'd been terribly convincing tonight!' laughed Hannah.

He took her into his arms, almost like a brother. 'You can't kid me,' he said softly.

CHAPTER ELEVEN

HANNAH now threw all her energies into the hospital at San Agustín. She knew that the only alternative was to go and live with Felipe—he had not stopped asking. But apart from the fact that Inés would be coming back, Hannah had been independent too long. She longed for affection, and Felipe was offering that. But her pride made her refuse. She would bear her hurt, and her desperate need—alone.

The nurses, Raquel and Esteban had been wonderful. Although the patients were slow to come back, every day they found something new to do. They gave the place a good spring-clean inside, and Esteban and some friends painted the hospital outside. Carla brought down the old Red Cross flag, mended it carefully, washed it and made Esteban paint the flagpole before she raised it again.

Soon the little place was as busy with casualties as though it had never been closed. The operating theatre was seldom used, except for stitching of cuts, and excision of warts and cysts, that Hannah could do under local anaesthetic. It was good to be busy. Hannah pushed to the back of her mind her application to the WHO. They hadn't written back anyway. And her vague ideas of taking some time off to go to England faded, as she found real pleasure in her work again.

Rosita left, though. Her mother came with an injury to her finger. 'Rosita ask me to tell you—she is going to work in the Villa Pandora.'

'I thought she might.' Hannah tried not to be hurt. But Rosita had always shown that her loyalties had been to her relatives who worked there—and to their handsome young employer, who had brought justice and respect to the name of Riviero. Even though Rosita told her they only spoke of union matters, it had been plain that they got on well together. It was no wonder she had gone.

'If you need her, she will come and help out,' Rosita's mother assured her.

Hannah finished splinting the finger to the healthy one next to it. 'I am fine, *señora*. Riviero will pay better than I.'

The woman beamed. 'He pays very well—such a good man. Every month he promises that a conference will take place, and anyone who has a problem, he will listen. All the workers love Ramón.'

There was no more time for chat, as the waiting room filled up. Hannah was glad that Ramón had cleared his name. Only she and the Rodriguez couple knew the deadly secret that had spurred Ramón on to make the changes quickly. Only they knew how limited his time could be. So in spite of the shock it had been, she knew that all was for the best.

Carla loved talking over what had happened; she found it poetic justice. 'So you said the first words, and Dr Riviero stood up and said more?'

'That's how it was.' Hannah found she didn't mind speaking of it.

Carla said, her black eyes on her employer, 'And that is why you stay away from the Villa Pandora? To show that you and Dr Riviero did not plan in advance to kill Benito?'

'Partly that. And partly because we have very little in common now. I'm glad he's settled his troubles. He will be a contented man, now that his devil has gone from his shoulder.'

'I hear he is. He works on the plantation, and rides each day.'

Hannah smiled. 'So everyone says. With Juana Lorenzo.'

Carla was discreet. 'So the talk goes.' She went on with more enthusiasm, 'Have you heard he allows everyone to take a rest in the heat of the day, with no loss of pay?'

One day they were slack. Carla had taken to bringing her embroidery, after her skill in mending the flag had been praised, and Hannah was sitting with her on the hospital steps, untangling a skein of silk. Her work basket had fallen, and the embroidery silks become ravelled. They sat like two peasant women, chatting and untangling their work.

There was a sudden screech of brakes. A car was stopping very sharply. Hannah looked up without much interest—only to see the familiar black Alfa-Sud parked on the patch of new concrete next to her scarlet BMW. Ramón! What was he doing here? She tried to keep her heart from jumping, and having half stood up, she sat down again on the steps and turned back to the embroidery.

But Ramón was already striding down the path, kicking aside some small stones, and alarming a tiny sparrow who had been contentedly taking a dust-bath in the path. She heard his voice, friendly, cheerful. 'So, *señoritas*, you look very busy.'

She had to stand up then. Carla had not noticed him coming, and jumped to her feet with a little squeal of welcome. He was still thin, but the black despondency had gone from his face, to be replaced with a calm content. His hair was longer, making him look like a rakish pirate. He wore riding breeches and expensive leather boots, and a white shirt with full sleeves, open almost to his waist. The glint of his gold chain caught the sun. Several passing tourists stopped to stare, such a striking figure he made, standing casually chatting to the two women.

Hannah found herself tongue-tied. Finally she said, 'You don't often pass this way.'

As he looked at her, the open expression vanished, and he spoke distantly. 'There has been a lot to do at the plantation.' There was no sign of that dependence on her he had shown the night his father died, the night he had begged her not to leave him. He was assured, aristocratic, civil. 'I am starting at the factory now, changing all the routines. It takes time.'

'I've heard of your generosity,' Hannah told him.

'It isn't just the pay. The working conditions were bad. I must trace all ex-workers, to make sure they show no trace of pneumoconiosis.'

Hannah said with a hint of a smile, 'I'm grateful to you

for modernising your lorries.'

Ramón did not react to the smile. 'How could I forget your complaints?'

Carla said, 'Please stay and have something cold to drink.'

He took a step forward, and Hannah held her breath. Was this the start of a renewal of their friendship? But then he said, again distant, 'You are tempting me, but I have much to do.' He held out his hand, first to Carla. 'Thank you for the invitation.' Hannah put down the skein she had been playing with and walked back along the path with him, out of good manners. He said, 'It is good you are back at work.'

She said quietly, 'To my pseudo-medicine? Belly-ache pills and hangover cures?'

Ramón smiled very slightly, 'It is all needed.' Then he said, 'Rosita said you do not charge the people who can't pay. How do you keep in business?'

'The hotel contracts pay the bills—Just,' said Hannah.

'Good.'

There was silence between them, as though neither wanted to be the first to say goodbye. But then a Mercedes truck, brand-new and fumeless, went past, and Ramón waved to the driver. 'I have to go,' he said. 'I am to meet him there.'

Hannah held out her hand and he gave it a strong shake. Then he looked away quickly as he saw her fingers tremble. She hid her hand quickly in the fold of her dress. Ramón climbed quickly into the car, slammed the door. He gave her one quick glance before roaring away into the stream of traffic.

He had seen it, she was sure. She had managed so well up to that last moment. Then her control had slipped . . . Now it was Hannah's turn to kick at a stone, to send it rattling along the path so that it kicked up against the newly painted door of the hospital, elegant in dark green, to match the louvred shutters.

If only she hadn't met him! But all the emotions came flooding back, and her new-found peace of mind was shattered. For the rest of the week she was unsettled.

When Saturday came, she drove out in the new car, knowing very well that she was going past the Villa Pandora, because she had no self-control left to stop herself. She had no intention of going in; she only wanted to drive past, to see again the scene of her last embrace, the winding, beautiful drive, the lake with the flamingoes on it, the bright toucans, cheekily cocking their heads at passers-by.

She wished she had stayed at home. The gates of the Villa Pandora were wide open, unguarded. Workers were sunning themselves in the grottoes, feeding the parrots and macaws with seed, using the gardens as they would a public park.

And she saw Ramón with a beautiful woman. It was Juana Lorenzo—Hannah recognised the voluptuous figure, the glossy hair piled up on the elegant head. They stood by the fountain. Ramón had a white cockatoo on his wrist, and the two of them were laughing at what it was saying. Then he gave it to his companion, and she took it, clinging to Ramón with her other hand, as it fluttered and squawked to keep its balance.

Hannah started the engine with a jerk of her hand, and Ramón looked up at the sound. She knew he would have no difficulty recognising her scarlet car, but she didn't look back. She put her foot down, steering round the bends at a dangerous rate, in her desperate need to get away from the pain that was tugging at her heart. Why had she come, knowing full well that there would be no joy for her at the Villa Pandora?

She was at the hospital again before her heartbeats were back to normal.

The next time she felt like driving, she made very sure she went past the turning for San Nicolás. She found herself down in the harbour at Mogan. That was better. She loved watching the fishermen—and the richer yachts, as they negotiated the harbour mouth, tossed on the emerald and sapphire waters. Hannah parked near the wall, and leaned on it, watching a particularly glossy craft being refuelled at the harbour filling station.

'Hannah!'

Surely she hadn't heard correctly. No one would know

her here. But then light feet were running along towards her, and she turned to see the welcome familiar face of Felipe Piedras. He stopped in front of her. 'You look so well and happy, Hannah,' he smiled.

'I'm well. And happy to meet you, Felipe.'

There was concern in his nice brown eyes, as they narrowed slightly, examined her face more closely. 'But not really happy?'

'Who is really happy?' she shrugged.

'I am, comparatively. Would you like to come for a sail?'

She shook her head. 'I'm not good company.'

'Hannah?' She looked up and met his gaze. 'I'm not asking you in order to make love to you. Inés is with me. Come and talk, join us in a glass of wine. Please?'

'Inés is back?' She looked into his face, and saw assurance there that he was happy. 'Then I'll come and say hello. But I really have no time to waste.'

'That is an outright lie, but I forgive you, *preciosa*.' Felipe took her arm, and they walked together towards the *Titania*. Hannah thought back to her one rather passionate trip—thankful that she had insisted on returning to port before her conscience had anything drastic to deal with.

Inés came up on deck and saw them, waving her hand with a smile. 'Hannah, are you coming to join us?' she called.

'Welcome home, Inés. No, thank you—I only came out for a quick drive. I must get back to the hospital.'

Inés climbed up the ladder to shake Hannah's hand. 'I have heard about the accident. I am so very sorry.'

'It was only a scratch.' Hannah changed the subject. 'Your husband has been like a brother to Ramón. He was always there when he was needed. Everyone is most grateful.'

She left the husband and wife. Inés gave another friendly wave as she went. They seemed perfectly happy, perfectly reconciled—and there was no sign of Inés' mother. Perhaps Felipe had taken her advice after all? She watched them start the engine and ease through the harbour mouth before hoisting the sails. And as their craft grew small, and her eyes grew tired, the image was replaced by another—the image of Ramón, with a fluttering white cockatoo and the widow Juana Lorenzo . . .

Hannah went back to the hospital. The scene was as it always was—unchanged. And so life went on. Those couples were fortunate, who had found the right one in life, like Pablo and Dolores. They sailed on together, facing everything as a team, with no resentment, no conflict, to split them. Now it looked as though Felipe and Inés had joined them in marital contentment. She hoped so. Felipe—would she have accepted his invitation today if he had been alone? She had to admit that she was very lonely. Yet she would have been just as lonely—and guilty as well. No, she would not have gone. But the temptation was past.

Someone rang the hospital bell. Although Hannah did not have regular hours at weekends, she was open for emergencies if she was in. She opened the door. Pablo and Dolores stood together on the steps. 'Come in, come in,' she smiled. It was nice of them to call. 'Carla has left me some freshly made lemonade. Come to the verandah.'

They went outside. Dolores was strangely quiet, her eyes bright, but Pablo was smiling broadly. 'Lemonade is nice, but champagne would be more suitable.'

Hannah turned. 'What are you telling me? She looked from one to the other. The suppressed excitement was more than she could bear. 'Tell me, tell me quickly!'

Pablo came up to her and took out a piece of paper from his shirt pocket. 'Ramón's latest results. I had them repeated, so that I knew there could be no mistake. Look for yourself, Hannah.'

She took the precious paper. Her eyes suddenly refused to focus, and she had to sit down and steady herself, control her emotion. With shaking finger, she went down the list of enzymes and blood components. Each one was normal—every one, including the eosinophils. She read it through again.

'Pablo, this is so wonderful! It's a miracle!' she gasped.

'Not completely. The results had been stable for so long that I knew the decline had been halted. It was a question of when the upturn would come.'

'Don't be modest, Pablo. You're a superb physician.'

Pablo shrugged, but his face still shone with delight. 'What did I do except pray?'

'You made him come back to San Agustín. Oh, Pablo, how he hated it at first! But look at him now, among his hills and his plantations! I'm so very happy for him.' And she had to hug Dolores in her joy. 'You're on the way at San Nicolás now?' She wondered if they had thought of asking her to go with them.

'We wondered if you would take them,' said Dolores.

'Me? Why me?'

Pablo blustered, 'I haven't the time, to be honest. I'm on call as from six o'clock. And Dolores is on standby for AED.'

'Phone him,' said Hannah. 'Phone him from here. I want to hear what he says.'

Pablo shook his head. 'You know he won't be satisfied with only a phone call—he'll want to see the results for himself in black and white. You aren't doing anything tonight, are you, Hannah? You can do this favour for us?'

She had walked to the rail, looked out at the shore, her heart thumping. Now she turned round. 'If I were Ramón Riviero, I wouldn't want the news from a foreign female,' she said. 'I'd want them from my best friend.'

Dolores tried to explain. 'But, Hannah, you were with him during his very worst time. We thought it only right that you see him at the moment of joy. He's given you a rough time—you know he has.'

Hannah swallowed, her thoughts hard to control. 'Even if I agree . . .'

Pablo took a clean envelope from his pocket. 'Thank you, Hannah. This is his own copy. See? Dr R. Riviero, Santa Teresa's Hospital, Las Palmas. I have to leave it in your hands, Hannah. How long you wait before taking it is entirely your affair.' He beamed again, and gave her a hug. '*Buenas tardes*. Ask him to ring me after the weekend to arrange the celebrations!'

Hannah watched them hurry to the car, pretending they were in a hurry. Tears came to her eyes. The Fiat raised a cloud of dust as it swerved into the Las Palmas traffic. She clutched the small hospital envelope in her hand, crumpling it in her joy. She had to take it—and as soon as possible. As a physician, it was her duty to give Ramón the news at once, no matter how many beautiful women surrounded him.

She couldn't keep still, looking down repeatedly at the envelope. What a plain wrapper for the gift of life! Then practical matters took over her mind: shower because you're hot and sticky. Wear something easy to drive in, because you'll be in a hurry. And have something to eat—you don't want to flake out yourself when on such an errand.

In half an hour she was at the wheel of the BMW. She was clean and fresh in a simple grey silk dress, with long sleeves as she would be returning in the dark. She had managed to eat a sandwich. And in her right-hand pocket was the precious envelope.

On the way she stopped to fill up with petrol. The garage man took his time, and she sat wondering exactly what words to use when she met Ramón. Would she just drive straight in? The light was fading now; perhaps the gates were locked at dusk. She tried to imagine his face when she gave him the news. She would say, 'Pablo brought this, Ramón. He wanted you to have it as soon as possible . . .'

And he would tear open the envelope. His dark eyes would be hidden by his eyebrows as he scanned down the list . . . And then he would know that he had recovered, that he was no longer under sentence of a slow wasting death.

Hannah turned on the radio as she took the San Nicolás turning. The dance music danced with her heart. The sun was just going down behind the cliffs, the valley mellow in the last rays, lighting the orange roofs of San Nicolás. Most workmen were going home now. The roads were quiet. Smells of cooking rose from the small square homes. She soon was turning into the narrow road that led to the grand gates of the Villa Pandora.

She stopped. Now what? No one was about. The lovely garden was deserted, but for the peacocks, the macaws, and the flamingoes on the lake. She heard a distant clop of horses' hooves, and then Ramón came into the drive from round the side of the villa where the stables were. He was riding a magnificent chestnut mare, whose coat shone in the low sun. He was looking back, smiling, making some comment to the companion behind him. And there was no doubt who that was. The lovely Juana Lorenzo followed on a gentle-eyed grey, with a flowing white mane and tail. Ramón and Juana were in elegant riding clothes.

Hannah had got out of the car and now she stood, feeling small and intrusive. She had no right to be here. Yet of course she had. She had brought Ramón the best news he had ever received. She waited for them to see her. The message must be delivered today.

Ramón reined the horse when he saw the vivid red car. He knew who was driving it before he saw Hannah standing by the wall, but his face was less than welcoming, the dark eyes unreadable in the shadow caused by the setting sun. Hannah said quickly, 'I had to see you—urgently.'

He said shortly, 'We do have a telephone.'

'Shall I wait?' She spoke haughtily, unwilling to be spoken to like some unwelcome salesman.

'There will be a long wait. We are dining at Juana's ranch.'

'My message is quite short.'

Hannah was deeply hurt by this reception. It wasn't made any better when the woman clattered up, not even acknowledging Hannah as an acquaintance. 'I'll wait for you in the yard, *querido*.' She ignored Hannah. She was beautiful, middle-aged—older than Ramón, but with lovely hair and skin. The large diamonds on her hands glittered with every movement of her mount. Hannah looked back proudly. How could the Spanish woman resent the arrival of a humble little Hannah, who posed no threat, either in beauty or in wealth?

Ramón said angrily, 'Say what you came for, then.'

'I've brought something for you.' Hannah bent to

open the car door. She had taken the envelope from her pocket and left it on the car shelf. 'Something you'll be glad to have.'

Ramón's voice was very low, the tone cold and distant, taut with anger. 'I wish you had stayed away. I saw your car last week also, spying on me. Damn it, woman, surely by now you must have realised that I wanted nothing to do with you! I would have contacted you if I wanted to—you know I drive past San Agustín every day. I would have called if I cared about you. You have your Carlos in Mogan; I have my life here. Go to him, Hannah. Please? Go to him, and stop chasing after me.'

Hannah had the envelope in her hand now; she felt her hand screwing it up into a ball. Her voice was suddenly soft, vulnerable. She gave in. 'I'm not chasing you, Ramón. I only brought you an envelope.'

But he seemed to be struggling with his own thoughts, and didn't hear what she said. He pushed his hair back, as he used to do when he was upset. He suddenly wheeled the mare round, so that the front hooves swung within a few inches of Hannah's face, and cantered back along the drive, following the woman. The still garden shimmered in the last rays of the sun. Hannah felt numb, an outsider somehow looking in on a picture, a beautiful image that had nothing really to do with her. She flung the crumpled envelope in the direction of the guard's little box. It was addressed to Ramón; he would get it.

The numbness increased. She stood for a long time. She thought she heard horses whinny—the couple must have taken another way out of the Villa. She moved, her legs stiff, unwilling to move freely to carry her back to the car. She automatically strapped herself in.

There was no doubt at all about Ramón's feelings now. He was annoyed that she had been to see him twice. She tried to cry, but the tears wouldn't come, only a sad little moan. She started the engine, and instead of driving back down the valley, she pointed the little red car up towards the mountains, to the dangers and the fears she had once shunned. In her present state, she had no fears.

She stopped once on the way up—at the signpost

where Ramón had told her she didn't need to come and meet his father. She had chosen to go with him. He had kissed her then—one of his impulsive embraces, full of a caged passion, swiftly brought under control again.

She went on, up, round the head of the valley clinging to the side of the mountain and into the next valley, where surely no sane driver would go at this time of night. But she would not go back. She would not pass the Villa Pandora ever again. She would drive through that long valley, where once she had clung to her seat in fear. Now she went doggedly on, round each dangerous bend, bumped along over the stones and the potholes—feeling nothing. There was no view across the valley now, only an aching grey void that matched her own inner self.

She stopped again at a signpost she did not recognise. There was a choice of mountain tracks now, and she was in no state to make a choice. Then, in front, she saw a light. She drove towards it, not knowing if it might be a will-o'-the-wisp, luring her to some doom that she had no fear of now.

It was coming from a cottage. And as she drew to a halt, going inside the yard so that her car would not block the road for anyone else, Hannah remembered the lemon tree in the middle of the rough lawn. This was Abuelo's house, the cottage of Ramón's grandfather, old Francisco. Would he remember her?

She decided that he would not. No matter. She was on the right track now. She could go on, secure that she could reach the right road to get back to San Agustín in the morning. She knew he wouldn't mind her spending a few minutes resting in his yard. She opened the windows for air, and curled up on the car seat, her heart weeping but her eyes dry, her face impassive.

There was a tap on the window and Hannah sat up quickly. 'Abuelo, I'm Hannah. I was passing, but I didn't want to disturb you. May I sleep here? It's too dark for me to see the precipices.'

'You are Ramón's friend. Come in, come in. I did not see you at the funeral of Benito.'

She said hesitantly, 'No. I was the one who upset him. I felt I was responsible for what happened. I felt very bad about it, *señor*, and I——'

Francisco touched her shoulder. 'Please come in. You must eat with us.' Hannah saw compassion in his old eyes. She would have refused, but somehow his invitation was simple and sincere.

She climbed out of the car, scattering a few sleepy chickens and goats. They crossed the small square of grass together and entered the tiny white block of a house.

He insisted she go on calling him 'Abuelo'. As they ate, the ancient man and the slightly less ancient woman and the English doctor, Abuelo talked of the old days, when he was young and fit and proud of his son. He had been hurt deeply by Benito's love of money, and more by his ruthless pursuit of it. Yet there was a streak of pride, that his only son had the initiative to make so much money, own so much land.

'Ramón I was always close to. At first he admired his father. But I saw the pain in his eyes when he saw how the peasants lived, when he lived in luxury. Benito's one thought had been to get away from the land, never to depend on it again.'

Hannah said with a smile, 'Ramón now depends on the land with his men. They work together, and he treats them well.'

'I knew he would.'

After the meal of chicken casserole and sweet corn, Abuelo said, 'Hannah, the way back is treacherous. Sleep here.' And he pointed to a small alcove, where a mattress had been opened out by the silent but smiling Abuela. There was a rough curtain to give privacy.

'Thank you.' Hannah saw the old man would dearly like to know why she had come, and she decided he ought to know. 'I went to the Villa tonight to tell Ramón that the illness he had when he came home from India is now cured. I brought the results of his tests, but he refused to see me.' She looked down. 'I was—upset . . .'

The old man said firmly, 'Crazy man! Stay here, child. I would not like to think of you going down alone. I will get someone tomorrow to show you the best way.'

Her lips trembled, the numbness allowing some feeling through. Here, in the middle of the mountain peaks, on the side of a precipice, she had found some genuine people. She nodded. 'Thank you for your kindness.'

He went away to the bedroom and she soon heard his peaceful breathing. She lay on the simple bed. It was a strange place, strange people—yet somehow there was warmth and human compassion here. She closed her eyes. What made Ramón treat her so badly? The tears dampened the simple pillow—not because she was without love, but because she had found hatred where she had expected friendship—and friendship out in the wilds, where she had expected none.

She slept at last. And such had been her afflictions that when sleep came she could not shake it off. She slept peacefully, dreamlessly. She slept through the bringing of a cup of coffee by little Abuela. She slept through the crowing of the cocks and the milking of the goats, with their tinkling bells.

She went out into the garden when she woke at last. The sense of peace was amazingly curative. The goats grazed on the slopes above and below them. The vines grew up their canes in neat terraces, arranged to catch every ray of the sun.

Abuelo said, 'Stay longer if you wish. You look tired.'

'I'd like to,' said Hannah. 'This is such a gentle place.'

The old woman said sympathetically, 'Ramón was always hot-headed.'

'Don't talk of him.'

'But I love him, Hannah. I have tried to teach him gentle ways, ever since he was very small, and could only toddle, and I tried to teach him to say the names of my goats and my chickens.'

They sat under a lemon tree, the old lady sewing. Abuelo showed his age by falling asleep in the middle of a story about Ramón's prize-winning at school. Hannah leaned against a tree and dozed, listening to the bells of the goats, and the contented buzzing of the bees.

But the smell of baking woke them, as Abuela brought out new cakes and bread straight from the oven. Hannah pointed to one of the goats, with a curious expression and a black patch over one eye. 'What's her name?' she asked.

Abuelo told her the names of the goats and the chickens, as he had once told his young grandson. Hannah felt as though she were suspended in time and space. Nothing mattered here, except getting the milking done on time. She fed the goats, and watched them as they were milked, their gentle eyes large and trusting. One tried to eat her shoulderbag, which was made of raffia, and she shooed her away, laughing spontaneously for the first time.

Then she realised it was Sunday night. Abuela came out in her best skirt, a black handkerchief on her head. A cracked bell rang out from the little white church. Hannah jumped up. 'May I come?'

They walked together along the stony track. The valley was full of mist now, deep, mysterious, awesome. Hannah borrowed a handkerchief for her head, and prayed in the little church, stared at by the locals, but when she smiled at them they were quick to smile back, to make her feel welcome.

That evening she stood on the very lip of the precipice, unafraid. She stared down into the impenetrable valley. Ramón Riviero had hurt her beyond all belief. Up till now she had believed such good of him, but after this, she would never stay in the same room with him.

Even now, in this serene place, she felt her anger against him rise and choke her with tears. She must have this anger under control before she went back down the mountain. She must find that blessed numbness that had come with her up the hill. She must be able to meet him by chance, and not react like this. He must mean nothing to her ever again.

Two magpies flew noisily out of a patch of bamboo, fluttered handsome wings, then disappeared into the mists below. It seemed a peaceful thing to do, just to fall into the cushion of gentle mist . . .

CHAPTER TWELVE

Abuela came to fetch her. 'Food is ready. Come.' She made no comment about Hannah standing too near the edge. The mountain people lived their lives with the precipice.

'Thank you for all your kindness.' She stood back. The moon was already showing, the landscape unearthly in its beauty. It must be after nine. They walked back to the cottage together, and ate vegetable broth and roast lamb. The ancient clock chimed eleven. Hannah lay on the mattress, but when the old people slept, she went out again, unsettled by the altitude, the eerie whiteness of the moonlight. She walked slowly along the path. Tomorrow she must go home. Yet the pain was still bad. She was reluctant to return to ordinary life, afraid that the scars she had collected might begin to show.

A small rabbit crossed her path, too young to be scared of her. She sat down on a tussock of weed and watched the little creature until it got tired of that patch of scrub, and bobbed off in search of another. The shadows of the grass, the bamboo and the cacti were clear on the sheer wall of rock above her, so bright was the full moon.

She left the side of the path close to the rock and sat down on the very edge of the precipice, her legs hanging down. The feeling of being so close to—not death, more to eternity—was new and made her breathe harder and excitedly. It was a strange experience, yet not frightening. No, not a bit frightening, all of a sudden. Around her, clinging to the wall of rock, a clump of bamboo waved gently, restfully, in the slight breeze. The silence was tangible, beautiful . . .

Then, far in the distance, almost in the past, she heard footsteps, a rough voice calling her name harshly, rasping in its desperation. Crude hands caught her, dragged her away from the edge, so that the small stones scraped

179

the back of her bare legs, making them burn with pain.
'My God, Hannah, what are you doing here? Oh,
Hannah, Hannah, Hannah!' She was crushed in an
embrace that was more painful than sweet, because her
face was crushed against his chest, and she couldn't get
her breath.

'I thought I'd never see you again.' Ramón was crying,
his face tragic with no sleep and no shave. 'I thought
you'd——' Sobs stifled his explanation. He bent down,
laying his face in her lap, clinging on to her like a child.
Her back was against the wall of stone. He had dragged
her from the edge, but seemed to have no strength to
carry her further.

She looked down at his shoulders—always so broad
and sculpted. She had always admired his shoulders.
And she put out a tentative hand to touch his hair—so
matted now, and neglected. He had been looking for
her, then? Why? It was he who had asked to be left
alone. She didn't know, but she couldn't bear his crying.
She turned his face so that she could see it, and wiped his
tears with her hand. But her hand was dusty, and she
made more marks. 'Ramón, don't cry,' she whispered.

His voice was choked. 'I'm a peasant, Hannah—a
crude Canaria peasant. I've treated you worse than my
father ever treated anyone in his life. I'll never forgive
myself—even though I thought I was doing right. If ever
I forget what I have done—I deserve to be horse-
whipped!'

Hannah smiled at his unkempt face, so dear to her, so
very dear. 'You're no peasant.'

He turned away, groaning. She liked the feel of his
face on her thighs; it was warm and close and intimate.
'Try to understand,' he murmured. 'I'm dying, Hannah.
I didn't want anyone to fall in love with me—I tried to
prevent it happening. I loved you so much that I had to
send you away—to stop you tying yourself to a corpse.'

Slowly, real feeling began to come back. She thought
it had gone, but the anaesthesia was passing off, at the
magic of the words she had just heard. The sharpness of
her love flooded back. 'And now?' she whispered.

Ramón lifted his head. 'Even if it's only six months, I

can't bear to be away from you. How can I let you go now? I've found you, Hannah. Will you take what's left of my wretched existence? Will you try to make a decent man of me before I have to die? I know I can't go on without you any longer. When I knew you were missing, I knew I needed you as much as I need air and water.'

He put his head back in her lap, looking up at her, his lips parted, waiting for her reply. Hannah took out a handkerchief, the one Abuela had lent her for church. She licked a corner and started to wipe the dirt from his face, tracing each beloved part with gentle touch. 'Ramón, you should have opened the envelope I brought you.'

'What envelope?'

'I threw it at your gate. Is it lost?'

He thought for a moment, then he sat up and reached in the pocket of his riding breeches. The envelope was still unopened. 'Is it from you?'

'It's from the hospital. I brought it for you—your results.'

He looked at her, holding the envelope with the tips of his fingers. 'What does it say?'

The wind breathed a sigh into the bamboo leaves above them. 'It's normal.'

'Normal?' His sigh echoed the breeze. He leaned his shoulders back against the rock, side by side with Hannah, and tore open the crumpled envelope. By the light of the moon he read—white cells, red cells, haemoglobin, ESR—eosinophils—He said as he put the paper back in his pocket, 'Now I know why Pablo sent you. He knew how deeply in love I was. He knew that once I read this, I would have no reason to hold back from you any more. Useless man that I am—even now——'

'Useless man!' Hannah echoed his words, daring to tease him now.

'I know it.' He looked at her then, their faces level, sensible, full of love and adoration and relief. 'Oh, Hannah, my dearest love, I know it!' He leaned his cheek against hers, tender, unrestrained now. She didn't move away. He said in her ear, 'The point is, could you ever make anything of me now? Is it hopeless, do you think?'

'How would I know, Riviero? I've been too hopelessly in love for so long that I can't think straight.'

His arms crept round her then, and they sat for a long time just holding each other, listening to the gentle wind in the bamboo above their heads. After the storm, this was their calm. They needed the quiet together, to heal their scorched and mutilated souls. Time didn't matter. Nothing mattered now—only the feel of warm still, intertwined limbs, close bodies, and hearts beating at last very near to one another.

After a long time, Ramón said, 'Would you have—I mean—did you mean to—go back to Abuelo's?'

Hannah took a deep breath. 'If you mean was I going to jump off a mountain just because of you—I can't tell you. I didn't mean to. I only went there for the peace of mind I felt there. I was hurting a lot. But all that blackness looked very nice—the mistiness and the leaves, and not having to think any more . . .'

He covered his face then, shaken with sobs. 'Oh no, if I hadn't found you—oh no, and then if I read that letter——' He could say any more.

She waited until he was calmer, then tucked her hand into the crook of his arm, feeling the silk of his shirt against the hard muscles. 'It doesn't really bear thinking about.' She shivered suddenly in the warmth of the night. 'Love is funny, Ramón. Look at Pablo and Dolores. Even Felipe and Inés—they seem perfectly sane to me. Yet they are in love.'

Ramón looked down at her. 'We must both be a little mad, then?'

'I suppose you're right.'

He wiped the remaining tears from his eyes and cheeks. 'Let's go home?'

Home. The word touched Hannah's heart. Home, with Ramón. But she hid her feelings with a joke. 'Yes. You've got Rosita and the widow out of your bedroom, I hope?'

'Of course—where they never were. What will you tell your Carlos?'

'There never was a Carlos. I invented him, to hide how crazy I was about you.'

'I knew that. Yet you did get roses. You did a buy a car that I knew very well you couldn't afford.'

'Are you jealous? Oh, Ramón, no! After all we've been through—you still want to know which uninteresting man thought me nice enough to buy roses?'

He shook his head again, more businesslike this time. 'I told you I'm a peasant. Will you please try to knock it out of me? I'll try every minute of every day not to be a bastard.'

He stood up then, and bent to lift her with him. Tall, erect, his white shirt smirched with dust, still in his riding clothes—Hannah gazed at him, hardly daring to think that he had declared so much already. She would have settled for just some of his affection. But to have it all, and to have it in such measure, was a treasure she would carry with her for the rest of her life. 'I'll try too,' she promised.

'You don't need to try. Just be your sweet self.' He put an arm, strong and protective, around her, as they walked together, with Ramón on the precipice side.

'Dolores once warned me not to love you,' Hannah told him.

'Dolores better mind her own business!' He drew her closer. 'You are still shaking, darling. Oh, Hannah—I know, I know. So near the edge—so near to slipping away from me . . .' They stopped and held each other, unable to bear the agony of what might have happened.

'We won't need to tell anyone where you found me,' she whispered.

'I swear it.'

They reached the cottage. Abuelo still slept peacefully, his rhythmic snores coming from the bedroom. Ramón's car was parked next to hers. It seemed so natural. They would go home in his, send a man to collect hers.

There was no discussion about where to sleep. Ramón lifted her into his arms, laid her down on the mattress, and slowly removed her dress and briefs. His eyes already making love to her, he laid his own clothes on the chair, and, trembling at first, took her to him, as close as a man and a woman can be, once, twice, three times before they slept, clasped tightly in one another's arms.

When Hannah awoke, it was with a feeling she used to have as a child on Christmas morning. She remembered what had happened before she opened her eyes, as her body and soul glowed with the glory of fulfilment. She stayed for a moment with her eyes still closed, waiting for the joy she knew was to come. 'Wake up, woman!' He knelt and brushed her cheek with his lips. He was in a stream of new sunlight, already dressed, his hair still damp from washing, his face shaved and smelling of soap.

She looked up at him, knowing the greatest happiness of her whole life. 'Ramón.' She held out her arms, and he went to her wordlessly. 'I love you.' He kissed her with extreme gentleness, making her recall the roughness of his embrace the time he bruised her. Now they had time—all the time in the world—to make up for that.

'Here—Abuela has made us coffee. I told her we would breakfast at home.' At home. She was to enter the Villa Pandora at his side. She sat up and looked for her dress. 'I've brushed the dust away.' He gave it to her, and she pulled it on modestly, in case the old people came in. But they accepted all with happiness on their faces.

'God bless you, my *nieto* and *nieta*. God go with you.' They waved as Ramón took the wheel. Ramón and Hannah talked as they descended the mountains, talked as they had never been able to talk, naturally and lovingly. When Hannah said so, he retorted, 'How else could I speak? If I had been honest, I would have knelt at your feet the first time I saw you, sitting like a beautiful child in your brown dress, your fingers stained with strawberries.'

'You liked me then, when I thought you despised me?'

'I fell in love with you then.'

She gazed at his magnificent profile. 'I guess we both had a very funny way of showing it.'

The men were already in the fields as they reached the valley of San Nicolás. Tomatoes, bananas, papayas, oranges and lemons, maize and onions—they were all being cared for, by men who recognised Ramón's car, and waved as he passed them. Hannah felt her throat constrict with tears of happiness.

They drove in through the open gates, along the beautiful drive. He left the engine running, and Gabrielo beckoned someone to take the car away as Ramón helped Hannah from the other door. They were all smiling and nodding at the couple, as though they had known all along . . . Gabrielo came back, and Ramón said, 'We'll have breakfast by the pool.' He took her hand as they walked through the cool house. Maybe she would get used to it in time.

He pointed out some empty rooms. 'This wing isn't being used. I thought perhaps we might open it as a clinic. Both work here?'

'That's a wonderful idea!' smiled Hannah.

'I couldn't have ideas like that until now.'

She squeezed his hand. They went out to the back garden, where a white table was being set. There was a smell of newly ground coffee. Ramón led her along one of the paths, to a spot where they could see the blue mountains between two tall palms, the blue mountains where they had just been. Ramón said, 'Shall we tell our son he was conceived on a mountain top?'

She looked up at him, knowing that he was right, that she already carried a child. 'Why not?'

They sat in the warm sunshine, saying little now, in the wonder of events happening so quickly. Ramón said, 'I'll never forget your face when I told you—God forgive me—to leave me alone.'

'Is that why you came looking?'

'Yes. I sent Juana home the back way, and followed you. But I went down to Mogan first. I never dreamed you would go up to the hills.' Silver trays were brought, with croissants, bacon and eggs, fruit and orange juice. Ramón waved the men away, and poured the coffee himself. 'I've lived for so long thinking that I was finished. It's so like a miracle, to be given not only life, but a family too.' Hannah put her hand on his as he put the pot down, and they grasped hands tightly. 'I'll never forget the sight of you on . . .'

She squeezed his hand until he calmed himself again. 'It's going to take some time—for both of us.'

'I'll never let you out of my sight, you know that?'

'You'll have to. I'm going to work.'

He nodded, with a smile. 'I'd let you take the Alfa, but as I'm going to the factory, I can both take you and bring you back.'

'That's nice.' Hannah yawned suddenly. Then she saw Ramón's eyes teasing her. 'Go on—tell me I can't stand up to a night with a man like you.'

'Can't take it, Day?'

'Just try me!'

They set off for work like a couple of children—a reaction to the ordeal they had passed through. Holding hands, they walked to the car. A long Mercedes was waiting. 'The family car,' explained Ramón, with a wink. His eyes shone with a glow that brought a lump to her throat. 'Me, a father! I never dreamed——'

Hannah was an hour late opening the hospital. Ramón dropped her off. 'I might come and have lunch with you,' he told her.

She bent and kissed his cheek. 'Once you're round that bend, I'm going to think the whole weekend has been a dream.'

Carla was waiting. 'Are you all right?' she asked anxiously. 'We were worried. Dr Rodriguez has rung twice.'

'I'm very well, Carla.' Hannah looked at the old familiar places . . . How beautiful it all was, clothed as it was in little pink clouds of happiness . . . 'Shall we start?'

The patients stopped coming at about midday. Carla said, 'Shall I go to Pepe's?'

A masculine voice interrupted. 'Why don't I take you both to Pepe's?'

Hannah turned. 'I didn't hear the car.' She gazed at him. He was still real.

Ramón smiled. 'I coasted in to surprise you.' He

walked up to Hannah, caught her round the waist, and kissed her soundly. Carla gaped. 'I called on a friend of mine for this.' He took a small box out of his pocket and produced a huge diamond solitaire. 'It should fit—I studied your finger at breakfast.' He slipped it on for her, and kissed her again.

Carla said in a hushed voice, 'You are going to be married!'

There was no need to confirm it: their faces said everything. Ramón put an arm round Carla as well as Hannah, and they walked down the beach path together. At Pepe's, the man who missed nothing was beaming with delight. 'Lunch is free. I am so happy for little Dr Hannah. Some days she sits here, looking so sad. Now she is happy, so Pepe is happy.'

Ramón looked at her, his face remembering who had made her so sad. It was too public a place to say anything, but they held hands for a while, showing they understood. Ramón said, 'Pepe, you must close up for the wedding, you know.'

That afternoon Hannah was glad she was busy, otherwise she couldn't have borne to wait again for Ramón. She kept looking at the clock between patients, trying to guess when he would arrive. She was seeing her last patient when she heard his voice, talking to Esteban. She was stitching a child's cut hand, and dared not look up, but she heard his quiet, professional greeting, '*Buenas tardes*, Dr Day.'

She looked up between stitches, keeping her own voice sedate with an effort. '*Buenas tardes*, Dr Riviero.'

But as the child was led away, she was already in his arms. 'Dr Day, how I've missed you!' Between kisses, he told her, 'I've been in touch with Dr Arora, and he's willing to rent this place. We can start planning the Riviero Clinic.'

'I hope you've been in touch with Pablo,' said Hannah.

'Of course. I went along to the hospital to see them. They showed no surprise at the engagement.' He looked deep into her eyes. 'They think you just brought the report, and I proposed to you.'

'Let them think that.' They stood for a moment. No one would ever know their secret. Then Hannah said, 'Shall we go home? I've packed some clothes.'

Ramón flung her bag in the Mercedes and drove round the winding coast, the low sun on their faces as they turned off on the San Nicolás road.

The entire staff of the Villa and several plantation workers were waiting to greet them, cheering and waving, lining the drive from gates to front door. Ramón introduced Hannah to them all, and she was welcomed with handshakes and with gifts, and with bunches of flowers. 'This is my cook, Hannah—Adriana. Now you see how much I love you—actually allowing you into my kitchen?'

'Oh, Riviero, that's true love indeed!' laughed Hannah.

And to the delight of the staff, they stopped and embraced warmly. Ramón whispered, 'You know, darling, everyone we met today thought us perfectly normal. Only you and I know how crazy we are.'

She pulled him down for a kiss. 'That's our secret.'

That evening they walked in the garden, the hugeness of what had happened again overwhelming them. The scent of the flowers was exquisite. They were sitting on a wooden seat when they heard a car. Felipe Piedras came striding across the lawns towards them.

'So, my old Knight—you seem to have lost your Sorrowful Countenance.'

'Felipe! I should have phoned you . . .'

'It doesn't matter. I just came to wish you joy—and to bring this.' Felipe pulled an airmail envelope from his pocket. 'Hannah, I have to confess—I didn't post it for you. I thought you were too unhappy to know your own mind.'

She took the letter. 'You were right, Felipe. But maybe one of our sons might go and do some good in India or Africa.'

'Or even one of our daughters.' As Felipe and Hannah looked at Ramón he shrugged his shoulders. 'You see, I'm not even a chauvinist any more.'

Felipe saw the look between the lovers. 'I can see

when I'm not wanted. Good night, my friends.' Ramón turned to Felipe and they gripped hands hard. Then Felipe turned and ran back to his car.

Hannah went to the lake and sat on the stone rim of it, looking at the flamingoes. She heard Ramón come to her, but when she looked up she was not prepared for the look of such extreme tenderness that its intensity was awesome. She put out a hand to stop him. He took the hand, but said in a low voice, 'My little wife, you have been through so much—done so much for me . . .'

'It doesn't matter now. We're happy now. Happier than anyone has ever been.'

'Happy? You haven't even begun to know what it will be to be loved by me—to be treasured by me.' He sat beside her on the wall, and she leaned her head on his shoulder. He stroked her hair very gently, playing with it between his fingers, then he laid his cheek against her forehead. 'So precious you are to me . . . so very precious . . .' He looked out over the lake. 'If I lost all this tomorrow, so long as I had you, I would still be happy. You know that?'

'I know that,' she whispered.

A demoiselle crane flapped scarlet wings and flew across the lake, scattering the moonlight, settling in the darkness of the cypresses. 'Come.' Ramón put his hand gently on Hannah's shoulder. 'It's time to go in.'

Part one in the gripping Savage saga.

When genteel Melody van der Veer is first deprived of her husband (and her home in England) by a jealous murderer and, subsequently, her freedom by American slave traders, she believes she has nothing else to lose.

But she is wrong. Soon she would lose all: heart, body and soul, to a fiery New Zealander and his war torn, windswept land.

An exciting new novel by popular author Hazel Smith.

Available January 1988. Price: £2.95

W**●**RLDWIDE